LOSS
OF REASON

miles a. maxwell

B B BROADINGTON
CHEYENNE / PHOENIX

B B Broadington LLC
Phoenix / Cheyenne
Visit Broadington.com

First Printing 2015.
Printed in the United States of America.

Library of Congress Cataloging-in-Publication
Control Number for Trade edition: 2015934114

ISBN 978-1-943054-01-5

10 9 8 7 6 5 4 3 2 1

LOSS
OF REASON

1

Family

Cynthia Reveal held onto her brother Everon a little longer than usual as they said goodbye. She watched him turn and wave with that ironic smile, then a moment later disappear into the terminal where his jet was parked. Why did she have the strange feeling—

She shook it off. *He'll be fine.*

Cyn slid into the corner of the back seat as her cab pulled away from the curb at Kennedy and tried to ignore the annoying squeal beneath the reggae coming from the radio. A streetlight's sudden illumination reflected her worried bright-blue eyes in the window. Her palm ran across the brown leather briefcase on her lap. *Should have told Everon about the report. But he was so excited, the new jet. Then he was on the phone. And I wasn't sure I wanted to say anything anyway. Maybe he hasn't left yet.* She pulled out her phone—

And hesitated. *No—Franklin! That's who I should talk to about it. I know something terrible's going on at the bank. His church—*

She frantically dialed her younger brother's number.

A fast busy. She tried again. The phone lay there dead against her ear. She checked to make sure it was working. Cynthia had her boss's home number on Long Island—

She stopped. Put the phone down.

I'm being paranoid. First thing tomorrow morning.

As they turned onto the Belt Parkway, the driver twisted the radio dial back and forth and the squeal just got worse.

"What is *wrong* with your radio?" She couldn't take any more. "What's *with* that sound?"

The radio cut off.

"Thanks."

She'd be home two hours later than usual tonight and Steve would be waiting. She dialed his number. After a single ring the damn thing disconnected. She tried him again, watching the lighted windows of Brooklyn, the Parkway high-rises set so close together. On their way to the airport, Cyn's older brother had once again suggested they escape *"this claustrophobic mess,"* as Everon put it. *If only I could talk Steve into packing up Melissa, all our stuff "and just get the hell out."* The phone disconnected a third try. She gave up.

Unlike Everon, her own work would have to be near a major city. *Vegas can't be all that much better, can it? The pay would be less.* She'd seen those tract homes on top of one another. The small lots—*your neighbor's late-night trash-to-the-curb excursions waking you up. Just like here in New York. Maybe there's a place for us around Spring Valley. Maybe I should talk with Grandma Del . . .*

She found herself jerked awake in a traffic jam. *What the hell? Central Park South?* They were blocks off the usual route, what she owed on the cab's meter way up—going *east* in front of the New York Plaza.

"Hey!" Cynthia said. "How'd we get over here?"

"Sorry. I had to go around. Construction."

Another taxi driver, head out the window, screamed at the car blocking their path, motioning with a hand gesture rude anywhere but New York City. Horns honked uselessly.

Cynthia angled her watch to the light. *Seven-thirty? If we could just go somewhere like the little town where Franklin lives—a quiet place without all the damn traffic and taxes and rules and frustration—*

She sighed and looked up at the flags on the big old hotel waving in the cold winter air, white flakes coming down. Guys in chocolate overcoats escorted blondes and brunettes into other cabs, probably going to restaurants or movies or the ballet at Lincoln Center, Manhattanites feeling the excitement of another Monday evening. The air covered them in giant dandruff, February's first snow. In less than an hour none of it would matter.

Something passed *Penobscot*—the Coast Guard cutter assigned to break ice and patrol the harbor waters. The sonarman scored a tiny blip on his scope. Recorded electronically for eight seconds, it just as suddenly disappeared. It moved so slowly, the cutter's computer-aided sonar classified the blip as BIOLOGIC—an aquatic vertebrate—and removed it from the screen.

Ever since 9/11, one cutter or another was always on patrol in New York Harbor. Time heals all wounds though, a scab never as motivating as open flesh—and the sonarman too, discounted the blip as the movement of a very large fish. Erased it from his mind.

Penobscot continued north.

The *fish* swam silently past two small private boats, moved beyond the Statue, halfway between Liberty and Governors Island, swung east of the Hudson River. And northeast into Upper New York Bay.

When it reached the triangulated center of three transmitter signals—the fish swam faster, rising upward. As it crested the surface, a valve opened. From a chamber inside, not unlike a long scuba tank, highly compressed air blasted through a nozzle in the fish's tail. It rocketed above the surface.

For every foot gained, its potential was multiplied.

A little girl in a party hat, on her way to celebrate her eighth birthday, a dinner visit to the South Street Seaport, held her mother's hand as they walked along the pier toward the bay.

"Look, Mommy," she pointed. *"A giant fish!"*

It was the last thing she ever said; the last thought she ever had; the next-to-last sound she ever heard.

As the fish reached the zenith of its arc, opposing charges in its belly imploded toward each other at high velocity. Eighteen nanoseconds and it all became nothing more than a ball of pure expanding energy.

On the Upper East Side, a siren like the lone wail of a coyote echoed through some distant concrete canyon, filtered through Steve Montrose and Cynthia Reveal's barely open window. Several car horns seemed to blare in answering conversation.

Probably blocks apart, Cyn thought. But she left the window open. She liked a little fresh air getting back to the bedroom at night. The horns, the siren faded, and from the bedroom there was the faint sound of the jazz station she liked. Not clear though. That same annoying squeal all but blotted out George Benson's light guitar.

"What's wrong with the radio?" she called softly.

"I don't know, hon," Steve's voice drifted back. "It's been like that all night, all up and down the dial." The radio cut off.

"Weird night for electronic stuff. My phone wouldn't connect. I tried you three times."

"I know. I tried you too."

She slid everything in her briefcase into the mess of an open drawer, second from the bottom in a black file cabinet covered with colorful plastic flower stickers. *Out of sight, out of mind.* There was no way she was going to talk about it with Steve tonight. The flowers had been Cynthia's idea of sprucing up their office-nursery until they could find something bigger.

She turned and leaned over the crib that held their baby daughter and kissed her sleeping girl goodnight. In the dim light she was surprised to see Melissa's bright-blue eyes looking up at her.

"Guess I'll get that drawer straightened out when you wake up tomorrow," she whispered. "Nighty-night, sweet girl." She stroked Melissa's hair as her eyes closed and kissed her again.

Cyn kicked off her walking sneakers, hopped to the bedroom. She loved the feeling of getting out of sweaty socks at the end of a long day.

"Oh, I thought for a minute you were going to bring her in with us," Steve said. He'd just begun his own three months' leave as hers ended.

"I can— "

"No, it's okay."

She slid off her pants, laid them over the arm of the chair, removed her jacket, blouse and under-wear, laid them neatly with the pants and slid in nude next to Steve in bed. Pulled the sheets, the bright Aztec blanket up to her chin. Fortunately that sound on the cab's radio didn't seem to be affecting the TV. Cyn affectionately rubbed the instep of her right foot against the smooth skin of her Stevie's left ankle. Their favorite comedy was just starting.

"How's Everon?" he asked. "Did you tell him I said hello?"

"Of course. He said to tell you hi. He seems happy, his plant's expanding again."

"You okay?" he asked. "You seem kind of somber tonight."

"I'm fine," she lied.

He yawned, his foot traveling playfully up her leg. "I was thinking . . . think we oughta go shopping for a bigger bed?"

"Oh, I don't know," she laughed and kissed his neck. "This old double may be small, but there *are* compensations." She rubbed his left foot again. They'd been lazy about it—putting it off.

Cynthia turned her head. "Do you hear that?"

Time. Slowed. Down.

Off in the distance, what seemed like somewhere south, two sounds blended into one—both coming at the same time: one low and growling; one high, like the howling whining wind of a hurricane.

They turned—only a confused, beginning fear in each other's eyes.

Their bedroom faced south. The television sat to the right of the bed on the corner of the dresser. As the first pre-shock hit the building, Steve and Cynthia were drawn to an amazing thing: in the nursery, their three-month-old daughter bouncing high into the air, falling into the open file cabinet drawer beside her crib.

The fireball dwarfed the brilliance of what had been Broadway, fired the nighttime sky beyond the sun. In the first five seconds the shock wave traveled one mile. By the time it reached East 60th it still moved at the speed of sound.

To those far enough away with time to hear, the maelstrom roared, then sucked all sound to vacuum.

Out *Penobscot's* slanting window—as the sonarman tried desperately to cling to anything, a bulkhead, a doorway—he watched the horizon tilt. The cutter's stern rose like a surfboard on a cliff of water, straight at the George Washington Bridge. And then the nose dropped.

Straight down the face of the cliff.

Of the people in Brooklyn, Queens, Staten Island, Jersey City, Long Island City, especially Manhattan, no one had time to think about getting their car out of the parking lot to somehow make it across the Brooklyn or Manhattan Bridge and out into Long Island. Those bridges were disintegrated within moments of that sound.

No one had time to consider getting a cab to take them through the Lincoln Tunnel. Giant balls of fire blew through all the tunnels within moments of that sound.

No one had time to take their money out of the bank—or to convert it to gold—or to think about what to wear—or to decide what groceries to buy for their future survival . . .

Within moments of that sound, chunks of building from the other side of 60th blew through Steve and Cynthia's bedroom wall to join those of their neighbors on the north side of the alley, dominoing on uptown toward Harlem—

Such was the final destruction of nearly three hundred years of substantial progress—three hundred years of tearing down and building back up again—three hundred years of fighting over an island three-point-five miles wide and fifteen miles long; one hundred fifty years of planning, zoning and community boards, of racial warfare and welfare, of neighborhood scams, of gang war, corruption and decay; one hundred years of social-climbing parties of the inherited rich and famous, of finding-ways-around-their-squabbles land assemblage, of back room politics; and just over eighty years of building giant structures that reached into the sky, each a living breathing monument to man's greatest achievement.

Though the firestorms would burn on for hours, most of said destruction took place within moments of that sound.

There was worse to come.

2

Turbulence

"Waaaahoooo!"

" . . . I don't think . . . you're supposed to do barrel rolls, Everon . . . in . . . a . . . Lear!"

The night sky rolled around the windshield then the sparkled earth was overhead. The blond man's fingers on the yoke held their assigned altitude perfectly.

"Less than a hundred feet deviation!" he laughed at the end of the corkscrew. You *don't think?* . . . I'm *supposed* to do barrel rolls in a Learjet? . . . *Wahoooo!*"

And took them over again. *Free of meetings,* Everon Student thought. *Free of traffic—free of the earth, nothing but exhilaration blasting at 300 knots through the air!*

But Everon's attempt at getting Andréa Buer into the spirit of things wasn't working. That petulant look seemed to be growing more intense *and* to deny the intimate acts they'd engaged in only minutes before.

"Come on—relax!" he tried with her. "The Lear was developed from a Swiss fighter! These babies are certified to three g's but they'll probably take something like six. We're not even pulling a g-and-a-half. Enjoy the ride. How often do you get to really let your hair down at thirty thousand feet?—*upside* down?"

And over they went again.

It's perfect! he thought. *Not too big but not all that small either.*

He'd worked very hard to afford the jet. This was the payoff. He was actually going to own it! He'd flown plenty of jets—always for other people. *This one* would be his! *Well, the company's—but I'll be the only one flying it! And* it was time. He felt—*what was the word? Giddy?* He laughed and took it over one more time.

There were actually two things Everon liked about this particular jet. The joy of controlling such incredible strength and agility. And the eight-seater's best-looking female pilot he'd ever seen. He took another look at Andréa as they inverted. Deep brown eyes, long red hair that flew out as they went around . . .

Beautiful!

Granted, she looked better before—without the greenish tinge. *Maybe I better cool it, but this sure beats the hell out of flying commercial. I could get used to this!*

The jet belonged—for the moment—to Hunt Williams, an independent power producer—IPPie for short. Williams Power owned more transmission lines than anyone else in east Pennsylvania and west New Jersey. A fair number of generating plants too.

Six hours ago they'd had lunch, Hunt with hopes to purchase Everon's two solar power farms—one, west of Las Vegas; the other, south of Phoenix. Everon said he didn't want to sell. But he'd be happy to trade Hunt all the solar panels he wanted. Everon wanted Hunt's jet.

The older executive had already replaced it with a larger model, a Gulfstream. The Lear would be Everon's first.

The flight out from Nevada had been fun—a vague flirtatious sexual tension right from the start while Andréa took him through the jet's systems.

Sometime later, she mentioned she'd seen his picture on the cover of *Entrepreneur* magazine, and some other high-tech rag she couldn't remember the name of. She nearly purred recalling an old story she'd read in *Gliding* about his U.S. sailplane distance record out of San Diego. She said she'd been wanting to meet him for a while. Even asked for his autograph, which he thought was pretty funny. *That was a new one!* He'd obliged, scribbling on a napkin from the jet's galley.

She gave him a little peck on the cheek when he handed it to her. *A gorgeous, lithe female pilot with flaming red hair? It was only good manners to kiss her back, wasn't it?* To Everon, she seemed adventurous somehow, provocative.

But that was as far as it went.

Until he left Cyn at JFK for the trip back home. Then, headed west over New York State, they'd cleared the clouds, looked at each other and simply started kissing.

Things escalated. She turned on the autopilot—not the only thing that got turned on, her left knee against his right, a hand between his legs, up his thigh to let him know what she wanted. He returned the move. He felt the moisture building in the crotch of her tightly-knit pants.

The cockpit was tight but instead of going back to use one of the jet's roomier convenient foldout beds, Everon kept his position in the pilot's seat—to retake control if he had to. As she rose from the right seat, Andréa unzipped his fly, slid off her pants and panties in one deft motion, turned her ass sideways and engaged him—sat right down onto his cock, her fingers weaving into his wavy blond hair, taking him inside at twenty-six thousand feet.

Mile High Club? Hell—five miles!

Unbearably romantic, so intense. Linked together—stars above—more alone than two people could ever be on the planet's surface. Andréa Buer proved to be a wild, insatiable, undeniable woman.

A quarter hour later he thought, *Whew!*

Unlike the man who smokes or watches cable TV after sex, Everon needed to recover in his own way. Once every muscle in his body had released its tension, he craved something more to cap things off.

They were over Pennsylvania when he let loose of Andréa and took control of the plane. He decided to take the Lear up to thirty thousand feet, near its altitude of maximum efficiency—see what the damned thing would do.

But her sexual aggression had misled him. Believing she would be more adventurous after such a great lay, Andréa surprised him by becoming a real *whiner.* Now he regretted screwing her, and he was beginning to regret even flying with her too. *Shit! Does sex give* all *women the emotional confidence to whine?* He'd never thought so. He leveled out to the tinkling crash of a glass breaking somewhere back in the cabin.

Shit, he frowned at her, "You okay?"

She nodded and gulped, glaring at him, "Please don't do that again—*sir.*"

"Hey! What's this *sir* stuff?"

Before she could answer, the right wing dipped hard. She shot him an angry glance, thinking *what an asshole* he was for ignoring her feelings. But the yoke was still level. He had a death grip on it and hadn't done a damn thing.

"What the hell!" he said as the plane continued to nose over, bucking violently. Everon twisted, pulled at the yoke, trying to bring the nose up.

It appeared to be completely out of his control.

3

Into The Dirt

His hand beat hers by a second pulling the turbines' power back to zero. The airspeed indicator was already in the red.

Andréa, seeing his reaction, added her strength to his, pulling back on her own yoke from the right seat.

But the controls seemed to have their own idea. Hurling them vertically toward the ground, now down to twenty-eight thousand feet—pulling on the controls face down, hanging against seat straps that cut into her body—only preferable to being thrown against a windshield a foot from her face.

Neither of them said anything as they struggled together against gravity.

"I think it's coming up!" she gasped. The plane's nose slowly rose, its violent bucking smoothing out. Five degrees, ten . . .

And then another wave knocked them right over the falls. The jet's nose continuing *past* vertical.

Everon thought the wings would be ripped from the fuselage. The blood rushed to his face. He clamped his teeth against the terror flowing into his skull, pushed it away with one word: *PULL!* While the plane raced toward an impact that would spell their deaths in the dirt.

Eighteen thousand feet . . . fifteen thousand . . . and the Lear began to respond . . . slowly, much too slowly to suit Everon, but still, the nose came forward.

Air screamed outside over the cabin. *How much can the wings take?*

Extreme pressure on his arms, pushed against his legs—flight angle changing at a snail's pace, they rushed downward past nine thousand feet.

Ten degrees, twenty, forty-five . . .

At five thousand two hundred feet they finally regained the horizon.

"Hail Mary, full of grace . . . " Andréa muttered. She took a deep breath, grabbed a look at the flashing console lights. Reached up to shut off the high-pitched alarm still pinging from their sudden altitude loss.

"What *was* that?" she asked.

"I don't know."

"I hate to say it, Everon . . . " she admitted shakily, massaging her stomach, "it's a good thing you insisted we buckle these belts, preceding your aerobatic unruliness."

"I guess that *sir stuff* went out the window a couple miles higher."

She smiled weakly, "I guess so."

"See what you can find out on the radio, okay?"

"Okay," she said, picking up her headset off the floor.

"One-Oscar-Mike—New York Center do you read?"

Static.

She repeated the call. *"Nothing."* The jet's displays flickered.

"Cleveland?" he suggested.

"We're probably too low now." She switched frequencies.

"One-Oscar-Mike—Cleveland Center, do you read?"

"Oscar-Mike, Cleveland Center." The voice was weak and broken.

"We were just hit by extreme clear air turbulence, Center."

"We're receiving reports of same from all over the area. Say altitude and position."

"Level at five thousand. We took a sudden dive from flight level three-zero-zero. Systems functional. Do you have any more on what caused that air we went through over middle Pennsylvania?"

"No information on anything like that yet. No storms on radar. Wait . . . hold on . . . word is . . . Something in New York . . . stand by—"

New York? While Andréa scanned the instruments, Everon frowned into the night. Exhaled.

"Breathe, Andréa," he reminded her.

She let out a long blast of air. "I wonder *what*—? I've *never* felt clear air turbulence like that."

"Once in a hang glider," he muttered. "Stupid

flying below a thunderstorm in Telluride. Nothing ever in powered craft—"

"One-Oscar-Mike," the controller radioed. *"All flight plans to the New York, New Jersey, Connecticut area are being re-routed . . . more information coming in—stand by!"*

She looked over at him.

"There are only two possibilities I can think of," Everon said, "neither of them good. The more likely, and the one I'm most afraid of, is a nuclear attack."

"Nuclear? Could there be radiation?" she asked.

"Probably not here," he said. "Predominant winds across New York State are west to east, right?

"On the other hand, EMP and a nuclear shock-wave would extend pretty much in all directions— in terms of air turbulence much farther, much sooner. I'm betting that's what we hit, or should I say—*hit us.* I'm not going jumping to any conclusions though . . . "

"We're pretty far from New York!" she said.

"I know. That's what worries me most."

Illegal to use in a plane or not, Everon pulled out a phone and tried to call his sister.

Nothing! "Lines must be down to New York," he said softly. *No! As long as—maybe— Franklin!*

He tried another number. No response. The signal level flickered up and down on the phone's display. He glanced at the instruments. They were still traveling west at five thousand feet across Pennsylvania. "Maybe if we can lock onto a ground station somewhere farther out."

Ten minutes later he tried again. This time it rang.

"Hello?" his brother's crackling voice responded.

"Hello?" Everon shouted back. *"Hello?"*

"Hello? Hello?"

Franklin couldn't hear him.

4

On The Edge Of Reason

Franklin Reveal's cobalt-blue eyes followed the slender blue thread which held his life. It disappeared into the darkness above, illuminated only by the beam of his pocket light.

He held his hook knife against the blue thread.

One quick cut, he thought.

A long fall would be a good way to end your life, wouldn't it? If you had the will, the presence of mind, the clarity—you might actually enjoy the ride down before the splat.

Then again, you might not.

The blue thread was Maxim ten-millimeter dry twill climbing rope; Franklin felt the straps biting into his legs, the payout rope in his left hand as he hung suspended a hundred feet in the air, off the lip of his favorite rappelling site in southeast Ohio. Ash Cave.

A mile walk from a quiet road. Alone in the dark

park, flouting regulations, Franklin came to Ash Cave because he wanted a break from people.

He wanted to silence *all* the voices.

Huge dark trees below, his rope was tied off to three of the larger ones beyond the edge up top. Animals growled and hooted. *Maybe one of them will just chew through it.*

A gigantic shadow of unknown origin fluttered across the remaining half-dome walls.

It's not a cave—not really, he'd thought first time he'd seen it. Eons ago, it was, before the cave's dome collapsed onto the valley floor. It was now only an overhang before a background of twinkling constellations.

Like his life.

Above the cliff edge, a thousand points of light glittered, more stars than anywhere else in the world—well, maybe not more, but more clear.

Bold rectangle of Orion, sword hanging down from the three-star belt at his narrow waist. Never afraid. Never conflicted about anything. Big Dipper. Primitive man drew an angry bear. Franklin saw only a giant ladle. Its three-star handle, front lip pointing at the North Star.

What will it pour next into my life? He looked from his knife, to the rope, again to the sky.

He knew why he felt so drawn to the stars tonight. February Seven. Today would have been his mother's birthday.

In the cold still air, a crazed bat fluttered past his head in search of a midnight snack. With a gloved hand, he pushed a lock of dark hair from his forehead, watched the bat dive down like some spastic fighter plane through the lighted circle on the ground around his Coleman lantern.

Bats? Like they don't know it's too cold to be out here?

Weird night.

Franklin rubbed a painful spot in his right shoulder, breath hanging before his face as he looked at the knife again, its lanyard hanging loosely against his vest.

One cut.

Why do I think of things like that? I do a great job. Help a lot of people at the church—

He chuckled darkly. *I ought to use my methods on myself.*

Where did it start? The seminary? Before? He couldn't pinpoint it.

Tonight's depression was nothing like those guys on the air transports. *Talking up that death-riding-on-their-shoulder thing—trying to prove how brave they are.*

This was new. This was gray. Not even the mission that led to his leaving the Rangers behind had caused him to feel so bad.

He'd joined the military to get away from the memory of a girl. He'd entered the seminary to get away from the thing he'd been party to in the military. Maybe he hadn't pulled the trigger. But he hadn't done anything to stop it either.

Now look at me—he looked up the rope again—*thinking about killing myself.*

The guilt still cut through him like a hot knife. *Thank God for Cynthia. Sometimes family is all you have.*

Part of it, he knew, was the warning he'd received this week from his superior, the church's senior minister. He rubbed a hand across his jaw. A dull ache in his rear teeth, just lately for some reason, when he spent an entire day at the church. *It doesn't matter—maybe nothing will ever matter.*

As he hung there, his neck relaxed, the ache in his teeth began to go away. The bad feeling slowly drained and left him.

"*Too* quiet," he sighed aloud into the chill air.

He peeled off the headphones velcroed to his fanny pack. They began to slip from the fingertips of his gloved right hand. Without conscious effort, his lanky frame kept itself upright while he switched the rope to his right hand, caught the edge of an ear cup with his left, pushed the headset comfortably over his ears. He searched out a local station.

"*Ugh—talk!*" *There ought to be jazz or classical somewhere*, he thought, twisting the dial. Tonight he needed something mindless.

"Talk—*again?*"

But the speaker's words shot out rapid-fire. "*Bomb . . . New York City . . . All communications out . . .*"

"*Is this real?*" he mouthed, knowing instantly that it was—

Everything stopped. "*Cynthia?*"

"—this special report. At this point we have only scattered information . . .

"Apparently, at 8:01 Eastern Standard Time, an explosion thought to be nuclear in nature originated near the city. It is unknown at this time whether this was a terrorist attack or something else. We are unable to obtain information from our affiliate in Manhattan itself . . .

"Damage is most probably extensive. Communications are down. Power is out. We have attempted communication on cellphone and landline, but circuits simply do not respond . . .

"Effects include all five boroughs of New York City, across Long Island and reach as far as parts of Connecticut, New Jersey and eastern Pennsylvania—"

Franklin's cellphone warbled. He pushed a spot on the phone's face. *"Hello?"*

No response.

"Hello? Hello?"

Static came back. Somewhere in there he made out a sound he recognized—

"Everon?"

The connection cleared.

"Yes . . . on the radio just now. Yes . . . probably—I

don't know. Right . . . Upper East Side. Perhaps . . . I *don't know* . . . alright. No, I'm in the middle of Ohio, camping . . . Yes. *Okay*. Bayne Airport's close . . . it's small, just a strip . . . in the *dark*? Okay . . . that's it. I can be there in forty minutes. I can— Okay." He disconnected.

His heart pounded. *Cynthia!* The skin on Franklin's arms grew cold. Strong scent of pine on the air. In his mind's eye he saw the bomb exploding, the fireball expanding, buildings going down . . .

Cynthia!

Abruptly he lifted the trailing rope, let it pay through the cam, barely noticing the service on his phone dink out, dropping fast as he could manage toward the light below.

5

Brothers Once Removed

The runway was too short, the jet's speed too great, its nose stayed up long after the snow burst from its tires. It plowed the air, struggling to stop before it hit the snow-covered trees.

The nose dropped and Franklin could hear someone standing on the plane's brakes as the trees came closer. From where his headlights barreled down the runway chasing the plane in his old jeep, it appeared the jet was already *in* the trees.

At the very last moment, the little plane spun, its stubby right wing clipping branches.

He left the jeep parked on slanted ground in the snowy brush, grabbed two duffels, threw a coil of rope over his right shoulder and rushed to the plane's opening door.

"Hi, Bro," came Everon's worried voice as Franklin climbed inside. "It's definitely nuclear?" A young woman with long red hair pulled the door shut, then slid into the pilot's seat next to Everon.

"That's what the radio said," Franklin answered as he tossed his gear on the rear seat next to him and buckled in.

"Do they say anything about any more bombs?" Everon called back.

"Just speculation that it won't be the last."

"Let's not *think* about that. Cynthia and Steve and Melissa are all that matter."

Step-brothers, Franklin and Everon were related to Cynthia by one parent each. Once nearly inseparable, the brothers had seen each other rarely in the last fourteen years.

Ninety seconds later the Lear's wheels left the ground. While hundreds of thousands streamed away from New York, trying to escape, Franklin, Everon and Andréa headed east.

Toward it.

⊥ ╁

Far ahead through the cockpit window, Franklin could see a sickening glow.

"Is this the *beginning of the end?*" he wondered softly.

The city on fire.

He closed his eyes. Balled up deep, as if his stomach were producing too much acid, he felt a sick knot of indefinable dread.

> *And there went out a horse that*
> *burned red: and power was given*
> *to him that sat thereon to take*

> *peace from the earth, that they*
> *should kill one another: and there*
> *was given unto him a great sword*
> *to make war.*

"There's no GPS signal at all," a worried female voice intruded. *Andréa.*

"Whatever satellites were above the blast zone must have been damaged by the bomb's electro-magnetic pulse," Everon answered her.

Beyond the fact that the explosion in New York was nuclear, they'd learned little on the jet's radios.

"Did you hear that?" Andréa asked.

"Can't make it out. Too weak," Everon said.

"It's so dark, I can't see a damned thing," she said back. "Highways, that's about it. Maybe we can get radar vectors." She keyed her mic: "One-Oscar-Mike to Newark Airport?"

Franklin opened his eyes.

Everon glanced back and flicked a switch on the instrument panel. A voice came from an overhead speaker. "Newark Airport is now controlled by military personnel. All private and commercial aircraft are directed to find alternate landing facilities at this time."

Everon turned to Andréa. "La Guardia?"

"Awfully close to Manhattan. I'd *like* to get the hell out of the whole area."

"Let's see what they say, huh?" Everon pushed.

Andréa called them.

"Turn off!" La Guardia's controller answered full of scratch and static. "All our runways are obstructed by debris."

Franklin wished he could just throw open the jet's door and rappel right down onto the roof of Cynthia's building.

Just to know they're okay.

"Kennedy?" Andréa asked, already changing frequencies, smooth jaw muscles tightening into a small bulge.

But Kennedy was being evacuated, already under a radioactive cloud.

Franklin felt each denial as a physical blow. He leaned forward between the cockpit seats, picked up an aeronautical chart from the floor. Pointed to a spot in New Jersey. "Can we try over here? TEB's an airport, isn't it? Looks close to the city. If it's not *too* close."

Everon looked from the map to Andréa. "Teterboro."

She changed the radio frequency.

But there was no response from that airport either.

"Look!" she said. "That highway." She glanced down at the chart. "We're here," she pointed, suddenly took the yoke and banked the jet on a course thirty degrees south.

"Teterboro area traffic," Everon called, "Learjet One-Oscar-Mike—anyone know if the runway is useable?"

Nobody answered.

☦

Andréa began an uncomfortable pass along the runway's right side. "How's it look?" she asked. "I—I can't see anything."

"No active planes on the field," Everon said. "I don't see chunks of debris or anything. The lights are pretty dim though. Runway numbers aren't too clear. A lot of dust, maybe?"

"No beacon on the tower," Andréa breathed. "No strobes. Runway lights barely visible. I don't know . . . "

"They're probably on emergency power," Everon said. "It's the best shot we've got. Let's take it." He called again: "Teterboro area traffic. Learjet One-Oscar-Mike turning downwind, Runway Two-Four."

Franklin buckled himself in.

Andréa took a deep breath. Turned forty degrees or so and entered the approach pattern—any moment ready to pull up. Not being able to talk to the tower was unsettling. If there was something on the runway, it could be the last landing she'd ever make.

"Learjet Oscar-Mike, Gulfstream Six-One-Six-One-Sierra-Golf, here. About six miles out. We'll follow you."

Another jet? Behind us?

"Okay, Sierra-Golf," Everon radioed.

"Cross your fingers," Andréa muttered. She pulled on the throttles to reduce power.

The runway was wet when they touched down,

and looked dirty. Andréa taxied them over next to two other small jets parked inside the airport's chain-link fence.

Everon hadn't lived in New Jersey for years. But he knew it well. It wouldn't be the first time the land surrounding Teterboro had been flooded by storm. It was the first time the result could be so deadly.

He had the side door open before they stopped moving.

"Wait here," he yelled and disappeared.

Through the door Franklin watched a larger jet set down on the runway they'd just vacated. Over the next ten minutes two more landed, parked parallel wing-to-wing with them down the line.

A dark-haired man wearing a black leather jacket, and a rail-thin woman whose straight blonde hair hung over the shoulders of her shiny red coat, leaned their faces into the Learjet's open door. Both probably in their thirties, tanned as if they'd just spent a week on a Florida beach.

"Anybody know what's going on?" the woman asked nervously.

"An Ohio radio station claimed the device was nuclear," Franklin told her.

"We know it's nuclear," a male voice rumbled behind her in the dark.

A sudden bright white glow appeared in the distance. *BOOM!* The sound hit them as it faded back to red.

"What was that! Was that a *plane?*"

Like a series of bombs going off, half a dozen smaller explosions followed.

Helicopters zoomed overhead, their spotlights sweeping for potential landing areas. People trying to talk all at once. Craziness reigned.

The woman had backed up enough to let Franklin step into the cold air. He edged forward.

It smelled of smoke and dust outside. There were more people behind her.

One man, face pink with cold, in a high voice said, "I got a report on a portable. The station we picked up over West Virginia said the Mayor of New York's missing."

"They think he's dead," somebody said.

"The deputy's in charge."

"Where's the President?"

Everybody started talking at once.

Everon ran up out of breath. "Let's go! Got us a small four-place helicopter. The last weather briefing says we've only got a few hours to fly in, do our own search—find Cynthia, Steve and Melissa, before the wind changes and blows the fallout back in our direction."

"Everyone's supposed to be subject to military law, even the police," said a dark-skinned man.

"We'll see," Everon said, Franklin grabbing his gear.

"Do you want my help?" Andréa said, as Franklin stepped from the jet. Everon didn't answer.

"You're going *in* there?" the thin woman in red called after them, voice jittery and rising.

But Franklin and Everon had already disappeared into the darkness.

♯ ✝

Climbing gear bags and rope slung over both shoulders, in the dim airport lights Franklin chased after his older brother, around the rear of Runway 24.

"Any danger of radiation coming this way?" he yelled.

"Wind's blowing away from us!" Everon shouted back. "Toward Long Island. For now!"

On the other side of the airport a small red helicopter had been rolled from one of the metal hangars.

"It's a four-place Robinson," Everon said. "It'll do to lift us all out."

Franklin stared at the big black tail number.

666KT. Red and black. The devil's helicopter.

"If we can find them," Everon added, climbing into the right seat. He began to flip various switches. "I had to practically buy the thing before they'd rent it to me. Took half my spare cash."

"Have you flown this type before?" Franklin asked.

"Not so loud," Everon whispered. *"Ten, eleven hours or so."* He hit the starter. With a high-pitched screech, the engine began to turn over. As its two long blades began to rotate overhead, Everon handed Franklin a headset.

"Hear me?" Everon asked.

"I hear you."

Everon scanned the gauges, adjusted controls. "Alright." He put his right hand on the yoke, his left between the front seats, lifted the collective arm off the floor, and began to twist a handle on its end like a motorcycle grip. The engine's sound increased.

From nowhere, a thick blue arm appeared in front of Everon, snaked inside and turned the key. The engine died instantly.

"What the *hell* are you doing!" Everon screamed.

A bright light shined in their eyes. "All air travel is suspended," said a clipped nasal voice.

"What!" Everon growled.

The light turned away. Franklin could barely make out the short, dark-haired man, right hand on a big hip gun, standing on Everon's right. He had a tight, authoritative look on his small mouth. He had tiny eyes. TETERBORO AIRPORT SECURITY across his blue jacket and cap. A silver name tag said VANDERSOMMEN.

"The controller's radios are out. They've got hand-delivered military orders. We're coming under martial law." He bounced on the soles of his shiny black shoes. Almost happy about it.

Everon exploded: *"SONOFABITCH!"*

6

Connections

From a minute after eight o'clock, David Niece found he had no heat, no water, no refrigeration and no public method of communication. He thought he'd heard the sound of thunder. But when he went outside, the stars twinkled through a sky that was dark and clear.

Nobody was allowed to build on the hills outside Stroudsburg, Pennsylvania anymore, but the house had been in his family since 1928—his only neighbor out of sight, isolated by trees and distance. The house was above the frost line, but his little gas generator out back started on the first pull. He plugged in the three thick yellow extension cords that ran through a hole drilled in the house's side. He heard the well pump turn on. He'd lost power before. He could run whatever he really needed to. He had a cord-and-a-half of wood stacked up for the winter.

But it was the fact that *all* the radio and TV

stations his satellite dish usually pulled in were off the air that really worried him. From his porch above the Delaware Water Gap, David watched a stream of westbound cars fill Interstate 80.

He got into his old El Camino and drove down the hill. Maybe he could find out what the hell was going on.

At the mini-mart, people jammed the aisles. Just inside the front doors, David kept out of the way, watched and listened.

Contorted faces, a desperation he'd never seen before, pulling hot dog buns and candy and soda and water randomly, fast as they could empty the shelves.

"Goddammit! I had those marshmallows first!" yelled a big walrus.

"You *sonofabitch!* You took 'em right out of my kid's hand!" a tough little guy screamed back.

Fists flew. Nobody—not even the store manager seemed to care.

And David pieced it together.

"My brother was just *in* New York, day before yesterday!"

"Anybody who was downtown is toast!"

"Shut up! My sister lives in Battery Park!"

"Sorry!"

"Anybody know who did it?"

He got back into his car and raced up the hill. *Shit! An atom bomb! In New York!*

At the top of his house was an attic stairway. At the top of the stairs he threw open a white door that bore a small sign.

TOP OF THE WORLD, it said.

He sat down and plugged in a black power cord he never kept connected—in case of lightning strikes—to the yellow extension cord on the floor nearby. He flipped on a speaker and began transmitting over his ham radio.

Ρ

Even on weekends, with the exception of three unemployed derelicts who closed down the town's only bar every night, the people of Marysville, Ohio—population 12,336—went to bed early.

"Ben! Wake up!" Susan Coupe shook her husband violently. *"Ben!"*

"Huh?" answered Ben Coupe. "What time is it?" Susan had the light on.

"Nine o'clock. Somebody's at the door!"

Their doorbell hadn't worked in three years, but Ben heard the pounding echo through the old house.

He blinked, squinted, pain shooting down his left arm as he reached for and missed a terrycloth robe hanging over a chair alongside the bed. A shoulder diagnosed with bursitis had bothered him for the last two years.

He slid his bare feet to the floor and pulled the robe on.

BOOM! BOOM! The pounding came louder this time.

He flipped on the stairway light and headed down. *"Hold on, hold on! I'm coming!"*

Ben opened the front door to find Cheryl—Susan's sister—and her live-in boyfriend Matt standing on the porch, wearing winter coats over pajamas and slippers, eyes wide with terror.

"Oh, my God!" Cheryl blurted as they ran forward. "Matt was up listening to that damned CB again—"

"Good thing too!"

"Shut up, Matt!" Cheryl screamed.

"What is it, Cheryl?" Susan asked coming into the living room behind Ben.

"Suze!" she yanked the front of her sister's bathrobe, "The phones are out! New York City's been bombed!"

"What!" Ben said. "New York? Is the whole country under attack? Who—"

Without thinking, Susan lifted the phone. A dial tone hummed back. "Ours is working."

ρ

At 8:33, Des Moines, Iowa time, the telephone rang in the apartment of Kim Martin and her two daughters. It was Kim's brother, Brian, calling from Canadian—a town halfway between Lubbock and Amarillo, north Texas.

"New York?" she said. "He called you from *Ohio?* That's a pretty close friend for an old college buddy. Did he say who did it?"

"Ben knows we do some nuclear warhead work down here," Brian explained. "He wanted to find out what I thought. The Amarillo television stations aren't on the air and my satellite dish isn't working. I can get one radio station, that's it. The President hasn't said anything yet—but look, Kimmie—I'm on my way out the door right now. I've only got a few bucks. I'm gonna hit the cash machine."

Kim ran with the portable phone to the kitchen for a look in her purse. "Shit!" she yelped. "I've only got a *twenty*, Brian."

"Girls!" she yelled. "Get your coats! You can wear your pj's underneath. *Girls!* We have to go somewhere in the car for a few minutes! *Now!*"

By the time Kim reached her usual ATM, there were already a dozen people in line. When she was one person from the machine, a dark-haired man came walking back toward her counting, and the person directly in front began swearing out the longest string of cuss words she'd ever heard, then turned and ran after the dark-haired man.

A message flashed in the ATM window:

CASH DEPLETED

PLEASE TRY ANOTHER LOCATION

That night, Kim and her daughters drove to three more cash machines.

There was no line at any of them. The first two were empty. She ran nervously from the last machine. It looked like someone had taken a crowbar to it.

Ᵽ ⲧ

In the middle of ten thousand acres northeast
of Burlington, Kansas, the head night engineer at
Wolf Creek Nuclear Power Plant studied a series of
computer readouts. *Those two rods on the Number
Three Bundle look pretty solid.* His systems were
operating near maximum output. *Good thing too
with this New Yor—*

He looked up to see a U.S. Army colonel and
four soldiers file in through the main control room
door.

Colonel Devers Broadmore introduced himself,
then announced, "By Presidential Executive Order
16-176, all active nuclear power plants are to be
immediately shut down. It is our task to see such
procedures as necessary are implemented effi-
ciently and safely carried out."

The engineer frowned at the colonel. *"Shutdown? What!"*

"That's right, gentlemen."

"But I don't understand. Why us? Way out here?
Some of the plants back East maybe. But us? We're
near peak load. If we—"

"Immediate shutdown, sir!" Colonel Broadmore's
face remained impassive. *"Right now!"*

The chief engineer hesitated. He thought of his
own house twenty miles away—his wife, his family.
Though none of the soldiers were raising weapons,
he picked up on a sense of increasing tension in
the muscles, the tendons of the hands that held
them. The engineer's jaw muscle worked. He took a

deep breath, then stepped to the main console. To the shock of everyone on the plant's night crew, he entered into the computer a series of commands.

Deep within the thick-wall concrete containment dome next door, motors whirred. An ear-deafening *hissSSSS* grew. Control rods of boron, cadmium and silver pushed downward, absorbing neutrons. The nuclear core's temperature dropped. Steam reverted to water, losing its ability to produce motive force. Generators slowed.

On the U.S. grid, the sudden gigantic power deficit forced switching engineers to make sudden choices. Like a pebble tossed into a pond, the wave of blackouts rippled outward into Kansas. Lights in ten—twenty—fifty thousand homes went dark as they were taken off the grid. Refrigerators stopped cooling. Hot water heaters stopped heating. Furnaces shut down.

At the Palo Verde plant west of Phoenix, River Bend north of New Orleans—at sixty-three other generating plants across the United States—the procedure was repeated.

Eleven million homes went dark.

In Marysville, Ohio, in the middle of their third phone call, the lights at Ben and Susan Coupe's house went out. In Des Moines, Iowa, the display on the fourth cash machine Kim Martin tried simply went dead.

It didn't return her card.

7

Frustration

BOOM! BOOM! BOOM! Everon's fist hammered against the metal door. He leaned back, looked up at Teterboro's control tower, a concrete building of square foundation, tapering six stories to the observation windows above.

That little red Robinson just sitting over there, he thought, *ready to go. Cyn and Steve and Melissa could slide right in the back and we could all get out of here. But once the military shows up—* There was no time to waste. *Have to get someone to give us clearance right now!*

He drew back his fist for another go when—*CLICK!*—he heard the lock unlatch.

The door was opened by a man wearing a blue bow tie and a brown goatee. A metal name tag on his white shirt said JOHN COATES.

"I need clearance to—" Everon began.

"I'm sorry," Coates interrupted, "no one is allowed to leave the ground. An FAA director was here fifteen minutes ago. She grounded all flights. The military's about to take over. Besides, our radios are out."

Everon studied the man in the white shirt. "All flights?" he asked doubtfully.

"Everything except military and EMS."

"My sister's in there somewhere," he pointed to the distant flames. "I have a helicopter. You expect us to just sit here on the ground?"

"Afraid so," the man told him and began to pull the door closed.

Everon persisted, not realizing he was holding onto the door. "That's *it*?"

"Absolutely it! . . . " he said more strongly, *"Sorry!"* forcing the door out of Everon's hand.

"I-have-a-spare-radio-I-can-let-you-have!" Everon spat into the closing crack.

The door hesitated. It opened. "That would be a help."

Two minutes later Everon was back from the jet with a black hand-held the size of a walkie-talkie.

"Thanks!" the controller said, widening the crack he'd been peering through. "Really appreciate it! At least we'll be able to communicate with the EMS flights now, talk in other pilots trying to figure out how to get in here. We've had six crashes in the area already . . . "

The blue lights along the runway's sides were glowing even more faintly than when they'd landed.

"Thanks!" He began to pull the door closed again.

"How long till your backup batteries fail?" Everon asked quickly.

The door stopped. "Not long. Our backup generator didn't come on like it was supposed to," Coates said.

"Maybe I can take a look?" Everon urged. "I know something about power systems. Have any tools?"

"Hmm." The door widened. "Well, I guess— We have an engineer on call but—" His words choked off, eyes turning to the city. He let out a long breath and stepped aside. "We have some tools in the cabinet. None of us know how to fix it."

Coates turned on a flashlight, led the way down a wide hallway.

"It's a diesel in back here on the ground floor. Watch it there, the backup lighting on the stairs is out."

Everon followed him past a handrail to where Coates unlocked a set of double doors.

The middle of the room was filled by the long diesel generator. Its engine should have started automatically—*already loud and running!*

It was silent. He pictured the dimming lights outside.

Along the far wall sat banks of batteries in steel racks three rows high. First thing, Everon looked from the big generator to the battery gauge. 112 volts. The red display flipped to 111.

"When it drops under a hundred, forget about ever starting this thing! *Tools?*" Everon urged.

The goateed controller swung open a wall-mounted metal supply cabinet. Its door looked like it'd been opened with a crowbar. "No one had a key."

It was a jumble of wrenches, pliers, a hammer.

Everon grabbed a screwdriver and undid a large screw on the generator's control box. Inside was a melted mess. The bomb's electromagnetic pulse had traveled up the wires and stopped at the transfer switch. The automatic relays were frozen solid.

He glanced at the readout. *109 volts.*

In the dim light, he looked more closely at the automatic starting circuit. The tiny black optical isolators had been turned into small plastic globs.

Everon studied the wiring diagram.

"I'm going to run your radio upstairs," the airport guy interrupted.

"No problem. Check on flights trying to land. Then come down and let me know soon as it's clear to cut the batteries. I've got to cut power before I can get this thing started. From the look of your runway lights, you don't have much time."

"Okay." Coates started to take the flashlight with him, not thinking.

"Uh—you have a penlight or anything?" Everon asked.

"Oh." The controller seemed surprised at himself. "Yeah, I guess it won't do much good— No, no penlight. I guess I won't kill myself. I ought to be able to feel my way along the handrail in the dark, I've run those stairs enough times. If you hear a scream, it'll be me falling down six flights."

108 volts.

Everon grabbed a pair of cutters. He'd have to bypass the transfer mains. There was a big spool of heavy wire shoved into a corner of the room. He cut off several three-foot sections.

Shit! Out of all of us, why Cyn? Married to a smart, good-looking, loving guy. Their beautiful new daughter.

107!

Hands automatically shoving old wires out of his way, stripping, bending, forming loops to replace them. *That helicopter! Just sitting there outside across the airport! The controllers have my radio. Maybe if I can fix this damn generator they'll let us go in there!*

He yanked out the shadowy mess of melted wire. Threw it on the floor.

⚡

If this works, they'll HAVE to give me permission to take that helicopter in.

Everon examined his effort, brain turning in a hundred directions. All he had left to do was bypass the main power leads. *"Where's that controller?"* He had to disconnect the master.

He glanced at the meter. *105 volts! The airport's runway lights are running the batteries down! A couple more minutes and there won't be enough power to start a lawnmower! Where is he?*

He checked a gauge on the generator's side. *Fuel level looks okay.*

The goateed controller ran through the double doors out of breath. "Sorry! We had a flight landing."

"I was beginning to wonder. Anybody coming in?"

"Not at the moment. You've got a few minutes."

A few minutes. Everon gripped the big breaker handle with two hands and pulled it down with a sharp bang. Now the airport was completely dark.

He flipped several switches. While they waited for the diesel's glow plug to heat, Everon quickly pushed the bare ends of the three wires he'd stripped into the relay lugs and tightened them down.

A door slammed out in the hall.

"This way!" someone yelled faintly from the stairwell. "In here!"

Everon ignored it.

"Okay!" Coates rapped a knuckle against his own head. "Knock on wood if you have any."

The double doors crashed open. Flashlights blazing, four soldiers in dark fatigues ran in bearing machine guns.

"Step away from there!"

Coates jumped back. Everon turned toward the man who had spoken, an officer with a pistol in his hand. "You planning to repair this generator yourself?" he asked. "Difficult to do with a gun in your hand."

"All airports in the area, by presidential order, are now under military control!"

104 volts.

"Well maybe you can get President Wall in here to fix this generator himself," Everon said with a bitter grin. "Or did you just come for the end-of-the-world tailgate party?"

The officer's face went red. His uniform tag said MARSH. Everon thought he recognized the shoulder insignia of an Army colonel. Standing directly behind Marsh was a face he recognized. *That asshole who stopped us flying in the Robinson—Vandersommen!*

103!

"Look," Everon said, "I don't know who you are or what you want, but if you don't get these guns out of my face and let me try to start this thing, in about thirty seconds there won't be enough juice to crank over a Volkswagen."

"He doesn't work here!" said Vandersommen.

Marsh squinted, studied Everon's face a moment, then turned to the man behind him. "Stand down." The soldiers lowered their weapons. He turned back to Everon. "Go ahead."

Everon flipped a switch. The generator turned over—at first rapidly, then slowed as the battery banks wound down. Everon shut off the starter.

"He doesn't know what he's doing!" yelled Vandersommen.

"Alright," Marsh said roughly. "Step away."

"Give it a second. The batteries are low."

102.

"Stop him, Colonel!" stormed Vandersommen. "He's damaging the system!"

"I said step away."

Everon pulled a lever, adjusting the mixture, tried again. *Rrr . . . rrr . . . rrr . . .* weaker this time, within three seconds it was barely turning.

101.

Everon frowned, reaching for the switch.

Marsh turned to one of the soldiers. "Take these men out of here right n—"

With a *RRROOM!* the giant diesel roared to life.

Everon jumped quickly now, manually adjusting mixture and throttle, listening as it went rougher, then smoother, then steadied out. He stepped to a master breaker and flipped the handle up.

"Check the lights!" he shouted.

Vandersommen stood there, lips sucked in, eyes tight, doing a slow burn.

"Go!" Marsh pointed.

Two men ran outside.

Everon's mouth opened in a chuckle that couldn't be heard over the constant noise. "You don't need to go that far," he yelled.

He stepped slowly around Vandersommen and flipped a wall switch. The overheads came on.

⸸

"Nice job!" he shouted in Everon's ear over the generator's roar. "I'm John, by the way, John Coates."

They shook hands. "Everon Student."

"You're not looking for a job are you?"

Everon shook his head. "Not at the moment," he yelled back. *Now they'll have to let me—* "Say, John, think I could ask a favor?"

John studied him, leaned in close, "Still looking for some way into the city?"

Everon didn't answer.

The goateed controller smiled grimly. "I doubt it'll happen but c'mon upstairs. You can ask Sue. She's supervisor tonight. She's using your radio.

"Don't slam the door," John added softly, pointing down the hall. "They've got guards outside."

Two steps at a time, Everon followed him up six well-lit flights.

"So then you're just gonna go?" a clearly upset female voice drifted down.

Just inside the doorway at the tower's top was a man with his back to Everon, his shaved head shaped like a watermelon standing on end. Colonel Marsh and two of his soldiers stood silently near a short, beautiful, dark-haired Asian female.

"We may as well shut down," Melon Head answered her, almost shouting, backing toward the door. "You should leave too. All the main radios and phones are shot to hell. What's the difference?"

The internal emergency lights were off now, the main lights working. Two flashlights no one noticed still glowed from atop a main console. Everon stepped over and turned them off.

"You can't go," the Asian woman said back. "FAA regulations—"

"Hey! You're single! We've got families to con-

sider! No one can force us to stay here!" He turned
to Everon. "This the guy? You fixed the generator?"
He head-pointed toward the radio the woman was
holding. "That your radio?"

"That's right," John Coates answered for Everon.

"Well, thank *YOU!*" The melon-headed man's
retort was pure sarcasm. "Beats the hell out of
the light gun—or throwing stones at planes and
shouting *Hey you!*" He stared at them coldly, face
pinched tight. *"Twelve* crashes in one night!"

Everon's eyebrows rose. *Double the number
Coates said a little while ago!*

"Probable crashes!" the woman said back,
turning to Everon, holding up the handheld radio
he'd loaned them. "At least we're getting their calls
now."

"Yeah," said Melon Head, "they start with ' . . .
Declaring an emergency!' then, *'Going down! . . .
systems out!'* . . . and that's the last we hear of
them." He was almost crying.

Everon could see the blue runway lights glowing
outside on the field full strength. There was no
time to waste listening to them argue. Cyn could be
trapped, maybe dying. He walked over to Colonel
Marsh.

"I'm a pilot. My brother and I have a helicopter
we can take in for a rescue mission. Can I get clearance into the city to look for our sister?"

"Afraid not," Marsh replied. "I have orders to
lock this place down. Only official Emergency Medical Service flights. The government has to respond
definitively to this threat."

"But—"

"Under martial law, a series of new emergency restrictions are being put in place for everyone's protection. Increased aircraft and airport security measures, tightened controls of highways. We're to begin regulating all traffic at shipping ports of entry, bus stations, train stations. *And* airports. Sundown curfews will be enforced by tomorrow night."

"Jesus Christ!" Everon said, trying to control his voice. "What good will that do? It's not an invasion! We've been bombed!"

"We don't know that definitively," Marsh disagreed. "There could be more coming."

"You've got millions of desperate people out there—just trying to get away from the fallout!"

"I understand, sir, but we've got to prevent looting and keep society as stable as possible."

"Aren't you setting up awfully close here? These hospital tents? What about the nuclear cloud? It's out there."

"Conditions are stable. It's scheduled to blow east all night."

"But tomorrow—"

"Let *us* worry about that."

"You didn't even bring any engineers or electricians!"

"We're only here to guard things, to coordinate military flights and authorizations."

"You see!" Melon Head yelled, fingers splayed, palms upraised, hands circling crazily. "They don't *need* us here! I can't *take* any more!"

He spun, leaving the room at a dead run. The metal door slammed hard behind him, but the latch failed to catch in the frame and it clanged and chattered back halfway open. Footsteps echoed down the metal stairwell.

No one moved to close it.

John Coates glanced at Colonel Marsh then turned to the female controller and shrugged. "Bob has a point you know, Sue. There aren't going to be many flights authorized."

Everon didn't know which way to turn. He had to find a way in.

8

Loss And Desertion

From the Learjet's doorway Franklin listened to his heart pounding in his chest and worried over the distant flames that lit the sky. *A million voices screaming for help. Is Cynthia's still among them?*

He checked his wristwatch. *1:00 A.M. and we're no closer to getting in.* He turned to his bag, dug out his portable radio and handed it to Andréa. It took her several minutes to tune in a faint and staticky station:

> "Pack clothing, blankets, sleeping bags. Medicines, shaving kits and cosmetics; infant formula and diapers. Remember to bring your checkbook, credit cards, cash and important papers. A portable radio. A flashlight and batteries may be

useful. Remain calm. You have ample time to leave."

Like Hell they do, Franklin thought. *What about Cyn?*

"Ignore rumors. Stay tuned to this local Emergency Alert Station for further instructions—"

The voice suddenly changed.

" . . . then at this moment, President Wall, the Cabinet, all locatable members of Congress are being transported to an undisclosed location?"

"That's what we understand, Brian. Goal number one is to protect the government."

"All right, then, Art. The question everybody is asking: *Who the hell did it?*"

"The FBI, CIA *and* the NSA are right on top of this thing. There are a lot of countries out there who hate us: Iran for one, North Korea for another. Syria. Even certain factions inside China and Saudi Arabia—though the U.S. does a lot of business with both of them. India and Pakistan have the bomb, but experts feel their involvement

is unlikely. We supply each of them
with thousands of tons of food and
financial aid every year. If—"

They don't know anything!
Franklin stepped outside into the cold and
shivered. He couldn't listen to any more of it. With
each passing moment, he could feel his sister's life
slipping away.
Cynthia!
He looked east, watched the unnatural glow
while his frustration boiled over. *New York's right
there!*
He'd never really understood fear before. Now he
did. Being *helpless to head off the vast unknown.*
Then he watched tonight's chance of getting
into the city go from bad to a whole lot worse: An
old green jeep with white stars on its doors roared
through the airport gate, followed by a cloth-cov-
ered transport truck.
The military had arrived.
Orders were shouted. Twenty soldiers disem-
barked from the back of the green fabric-covered
transport. They began to erect huge tents.
Franklin understood the military mind. *Order
and control. Things that will prevent us from going
to look for Cynthia!*
*But Everon's got us a way in! All we need is
clearance!*
His eyes were drawn back to the distant glow.
He stretched out a hand.
She could be dying!

He couldn't think.

Franklin walked behind the jet, along the frozen grass by the taxiway, tying back his dark hair with a spare piece of climbing cord fished from his pocket.

He sat down forcefully on the cold ground, lay back, put his hands behind his head and pulled his legs up.

Into a crunch. *One . . .*

Two . . .

Three . . .

He began breathing harder, rising faster. Down-up, his stomach nothing but a series of tight ripples, feeling his breath burst from his mouth in the cold night air.

He watched another of the Red Cross helicopters womp in overhead from the city. Imagined riding inside, going back into the city with it.

Twenty-four . . . twenty-five. He started over.

One . . . two . . . Franklin's thick dark hair came loose now, flowing about his neck. The same helicopter returned from somewhere behind him. *Landing.* A fuel truck roared up beneath its blades.

A few minutes—fuel up, restart, take off for the city again. How do they know who has clearance and who doesn't?

He rose and pulled down his leather jacket, heart speeding. He ran along the fence, past the unmanned security booth, through the airport gate. Along the chain-link fence, in the direction he'd seen the helicopter return from.

When he reached the corner, he saw a sign inside the fence near the runway's end. A notice to pilots:

> **Hospital Below Flight Path**
> **Climb To 1500 Feet**
> **Follow 040 Degrees Immediately After Liftoff**

The streets were littered with abandoned cars. A car drove past. And again there was only starlight.

Another chopper in from the city whirred loudly overhead. He ran, following the concrete sidewalk after it.

High on the hill, it slid overtop a large square building and disappeared.

⸸

What's he looking at now? The radio trickle chargers. Their small cube power supplies were black blobs of melted plastic. From the moment he walked in the room, the chief controller Sue felt bad for the incredible-looking green-eyed man.

He'd given up his own radio and now he'd fixed their backup generator. Despite the horrible circumstances, he appeared to be controlling his anger, doing whatever he could figure out to do. *Like if he can just fix enough stuff we'll let him go into the city.*

The city's glow lit the side of his face, luminesced his eyes. Two years ago, Sue and her three girlfriends had flown down to Puerto Rico. The water off the beach had been that exact same shade of startling green. So what if he was a foot taller than her own five-two.

"Hey, electronic genius," she smiled at him, "think you can do anything with our scopes?"

She stood watching his blond hair, the way the muscular California surfer build flowed beneath the tan leather jacket. The feel of him moving around the cabinet mounted in the wall. *Are his hands shaking? He's pretty upset about not being able to get into the city but doesn't know what to do about it.*

Well, neither do I! She honestly didn't really think he should go in there anyway.

He walked rapidly over and offered a quick firm hand. "Everon."

"Sue." She felt an electric tingle zip up her arm, down into her belly, almost glad he didn't smile. It might have killed her.

His eyes quickly surveyed the dead radar system. One of the guys had been pulling out square green circuit boards the size of serving platters, strewn them all over the floor—each a melted mess of chips and electronic parts. The way his hands sorted through a nearby stack of replacements, they looked like the wrong ones.

"Doubtful, Sue."

He knelt on the floor—lay down on his back and opened the access hatch. Movements rapid and sure, he stuck his head inside the console.

He has to know women see him as beautiful, she thought, *but there's a rough edge there too. The faintly glowing blond stubble, a one-day beard maybe. Lightly tanned skin, green-blue eyes shining in the starlight.*

She hurried her eyes away when she realized she was staring at his crotch. *Shit! I'm being ridiculous—like a schoolgirl! I'm a supervisor, for fuck's sake! In the middle of a disaster!*

"Fried beyond repair!" his voice echoed out of the console. "Not unless you have a lot more spare parts than what I see around here. The radar pulled in even more of the bomb's pulse than the radio system."

"How could that happen?"

"I heard about a high-altitude A-bomb test in the Pacific once. Took out a telephone system in Hawaii a thousand miles away. Engineers use high-frequency alternating current models to calculate numbers for lightning strikes. *Nobody* knows how to model the electromagnetic pulse from a nuclear bomb . . . " She tried to listen but almost didn't care *what* he was saying. As long as he was talking to her.

As he rose from the floor, his green-blue eyes locked onto hers. With a quick look to see if Marsh was still busy across the room, he asked softly, "Do you think you could do something for me?"

She gulped. "What's that?"

"Think you can get my brother and me authorized as one of those EMS teams? We've got our own helicopter."

"Are you *crazy*? The things you'll find in there— fire and thick, black smoke. The smell of death every way you turn. Radiation, buildings in pieces.

No way to get through to anywhere. I don't think
you should go!"

"Our sister's in there."

She stared at him.

"They say the bomb went off on the south end
of the island—"

"That's what that—" She glanced at Marsh.
"That's what Colonel Marsh told us—"

"Cynthia and Steve and their baby live pretty far
north," Everon replied hopefully.

She smiled grimly. Took a deep breath. "I can
try. I know a couple of the EMS guys."

While he waited with growing agitation, she radioed the team just landing.

"That's being handled over at the Med Center,"
the reply came back. "Our personnel's already set."

She felt a certain relief they weren't willing to
give up open seats either—they were reserved for
rescue victims. The blond man—Everon—watched
the EMS flight lift off.

"What the hell? Franklin?" he gaped through
the big tower windows. *"Where's he going?"* Everon
watched his younger brother down below, running
toward the airport entrance.

Things were falling apart. Like some horrible
pain in the middle of his back he couldn't reach. *No
military clearance—helicopter just waiting for Cyn,
Steve, Melissa. Now Franklin goes off somewhere?*

Then a voice called over his radio in controller
Sue's hand, "Six-Six-Six-Kilo-India, authorized for
military rescue."

Everon's eyes widened as he watched the red

four-place chopper he'd rented lift off and bank for the city, two men in Army fatigues in its front seats. *"Goddammit!"* His fists closed and opened. *"They're taking our way in!"*

Knuckles pressed against the cold observation glass, he leaned his forehead against it. He stretched out his fingertips at the distant flames. *So close! Cynthia!* He didn't know what to do. He could reach out and touch— It was so frustrating, he felt like *screaming!*

He frowned, pressing his right cheek against the big window. "What's *that?*" he pointed down on an angle through the glass, toward the low U-shaped building near the far end of the runway. "That building, with all the old aircraft."

"Oh, the museum?" she answered.

Around its side he could see wings and tails. He couldn't have made it out before, but the airport lights were up now—casting shadows from old fighter jets, a bi-plane.

"Is that an old Coast Guard chopper down there?"

"That thing?" Sue snorted. "That's Sam's pet. I think it was in a movie last year. It's just for display. I don't think it runs."

"How long's it been there?"

"I don't know. A few years, I guess."

"Who's Sam?"

"Sam Gunn. He owns the museum."

"Thanks!" Everon called over his shoulder. He went through the door to the stairs on a run.

9

A Red Cross Man

Franklin kept seeing *Cynthia and Steve and Melissa huddled together, trapped by flame and smoke. How long can they survive? Everon has the rental helicopter. All we need is clearance.* He forced himself away from the hallucination and onto the people around him.

The green marble floor inside Hackensack Med Center was crowded and crazy and people were anything but normal. They sat and milled about agitated in long lines and gibbered. *All I need is a certain type of person—*

Franklin noticed things about people. How they walked and dressed, their posture, the way they combed their hair. Especially their voices. From these he could guess things about the way they thought.

He made a rapid study through the intake windows, behind the counters.

Him? No. Her—not her either!

I'm not going to find the person I need out here!

At the rear of the ER, he found a gray metal door into the hospital proper. He tried the handle. It was locked. He stood next to the door's edge. *Can't be too long—*

Somebody pushed it open.

He turned to slide through, but a tall gray-haired nurse in whites blocked his way. She glanced at his black leather jacket, obviously looking for a hospital ID.

"Hospitals have rules," she said sternly. The door was closing.

Out of the increasing chaos, someone called out, "Nurse Vandersommen!" She rushed away. *Wife?* Franklin pictured the airport security guard. *Mother?* His fingertips caught the door's edge at half an inch.

Inside, it was field hospital triage. Franklin considered the doctors and nurses in scrubs, running around binding up bloody wounds, treating burns. *Him?—maybe—No! Him . . . ?*

Down a side corridor lined with temporary wooden cots was a big beer-bellied man, face framed by a pair of bushy red-gray muttonchops. He wore a white lab coat and a harried expression. *Is he the one?*

A printed paper Red Cross tag, safety-pinned to his coat, said CHUCK FARNDIKE, BLOOD CO-ORDINATOR. He carried a clipboard, seemed to be in charge of organizing emergency donors among volunteers. Including some of the hospital staff.

Franklin watched the way the big man moved.

Guy must have been a real dynamo. Something's worn him down. The Medic pin on his shirt. *Yes—*

Franklin walked over.

"Hello. I'm Franklin Reveal, a minister from Pennsylvania. Could I get a couple minutes of your time, Mr. Farndike?"

"Don't know I have a couple minutes, Reverend." Chuck rushed past to check a filling blood bag connected to a middle-aged hospital administrator's arm. "We can't locate our emergency blood shipments. The phones are out. Our computers are down. I have two people out knocking on doors trying to find donors. We're gonna be in one hell of a *real* mess around here pretty soon."

A young dark-haired nurse in scrubs hurried up to the big man. "What do you want to do about AB neg, Chuck? We're completely out!"

"Did you check the backups by OR 3?"

The nurse hurried away.

"Mr. Farndike?" Franklin tried.

Chuck rushed on by.

But the red liquid flowed as nurses connected empty bags to waiting arms of the few volunteers, each resting on one of the empty cots. Each time Franklin began, Chuck was grabbed by somebody else. He couldn't hold the man's attention. It was exasperating. Impossible to hold a private conversation. But this was a man who could get their helicopter put on the clearance list.

The young woman in nurse's scrubs rushed back. "No AB neg over there either! And you know how hard it is to find—"

Franklin could tell Chuck held his true feelings buried deep down inside: On the surface, his primary connection with the world was visual.

"I'm AB negative," Franklin said, to Chuck's surprise. "Hook me up. We'll talk while you drain." Franklin sat down on a cot and added softly an embedded command,"but I *WANT US TO BE-NOT-INTERRUPTED.*"

Chuck frowned at the strange minister with the long, dark tied-back hair. *Whatever he needs is important enough for him to donate his own blood?*

He nodded, opened a fresh needle and pinched it into Franklin's arm.

Instead of lying down, Franklin remained seated on the cot's edge, angled toward the big man at forty-five degrees. And began speaking softly, in deep, even tones, "You must . . . *BE TIRED.* Were *you AHH—SLEEP* when the blast went off?"

"No," Chuck frowned, "I was getting ready to go to bed."

"Hmmmmm . . . " Franklin nodded, dropping his vocal pitch half an octave, "easy to *IMAGINE* . . . a corporal I knew in the Rangers—"

"You were a Ranger?" Chuck interrupted, suddenly interested.

Franklin nodded, "This corporal, you see, was ordered along with the rest of our squad on a deeply classified mission op. I'm not supposed to say precisely where the op took place, but you can make your own guess—I can only tell you we were sent to a village deep (Franklin's voice went softer) in a South American jungle."

Franklin was nodding slightly, in time and sync with Chuck's breathing. Already, few hospital sounds were getting through to Chuck.

"Now this wasn't the kind of vision YOU DREAM OF, unless of course you were having a nightmare. This was a *very* bad mission. You might WONDER what made this mission so *particularly* bad. Well, the whole village, the entire town, was to be slaughtered. Men, women, old people, children too, wiped out, murdered, the way some of us saw it."

"*What—*"

"I *know,*" Franklin continued to nod with Chuck's breathing, blinking when Chuck blinked, Franklin's breath subtly shifting in perfect harmony. "I know. But YOU SEE, THIS PARTICULAR VILLAGE had been labeled by the-powers-that-be as an enemy of the United States. The coca plant was their number one crop, its processing, their only industry—mostly by hand, into pure white cocaine. THE ENTIRE VILLAGE made their living based on drugs.

"Our Ranger squad was ordered to fly in, infiltrate this area of highly guarded jungle, and burn them out. Burn the crops, the buildings, and, kill every man, woman and child, leaving the whole place dead to the bone. As if once the jungle covered it over, nothing had *ever been* there."

Franklin watched Chuck's eyes water, drift in . . . and-out of focus—saw the markers and changes in posture suddenly as he breathed in . . . out and *slowed . . .*

. . . *way*

. . . down.

Chuck barely noticed the tension fading . . . shoulders relaxing . . . dropping deeper down into his torso . . . right down into his legs . . . eyes softening, closing . . . breath slowing . . .

Chuck was entering deep trance. A voice interrupted.

"Chuck, what are we doing about AB neg?"

Franklin leaned in close. "Hold on a minute, Chuck."

"Okay," Chuck mumbled.

Franklin looked up. A man in bloody green scrubs stood there, dark hair, solidly built, face changing from urgent need to blank wonder—to a frown of concern. A nameplate said Dale Rass, MD.

"Give him five minutes," Franklin said in a lighter voice, pointing to the needle inside his own elbow. "He's pumping a pint of AB neg out of me right now."

The doctor looked from Chuck's closed eyes to Franklin's arm, shrugged, "Okay," then hurried up the corridor.

"We got on the transport and headed south," Franklin continued, voice dropping again. "Once we'd made our last fuel stop, the colonel himself— yes, a mere squad of thirteen was being led by a lieutenant colonel—actually opened our mission orders in front of us.

"He read them in silence, then stared into space. We could see our commander was pretty upset.

"Finally, he turned to us and actually read *us* those orders. He said, '*LISTEN TO ME CAREFULLY* and

CONSIDER THESE WORDS . . . ' We knew how unusual this was that he would share these with us, so we said to ourselves, *YOU WANT TO LISTEN WITH EVERYTHING YOU HAVE, TO EACH WORD, EACH AND EVERY NUANCE.*

"When he'd finished giving us every bit of information, he told us *we* had a decision to make. Not him—*us!* It was a decision to be made together.

"'*AS A TEAM,*' he said, '*YOU HAVE TO DECIDE WHAT'S BEST for the squad to do.*'

"Our *GETUS TRANSPORT, SIX-SIX-SIX-KI,* set us down in a small *CLEARANCE* in the jungle, whatever was required, and even though our mission deadline was one of limited opportunity, there we sat on the ground, our guns ready, while we argued it out.

"The colonel made it clear to each and every one of us that absolutely no action of any kind would be taken until a unanimous and unequivocal decision was reached by all of us.

"We could barely believe what the colonel was offering, so it took us a minute or so before we began to bat it around. Throw it back and forth.

"One man, a sergeant named Ben, insisted we follow orders, completing the mission-as-written. The sergeant stated flatly we had a duty to ourselves, to the Rangers, and to our country to follow orders-as-given. No matter what.

"But this corporal, hesitantly, disagreed. While not as high-ranking, yet encouraged by the colonel, the corporal said he thought our orders were in no one's interest. That those orders were invalid, unreasonable. 'Is what those villagers produce worse,' he asked, '*than sugar?* Does it justify *murder?* Worth *killing* all these *people?* Killing *children?"*

"*'LISTEN TO ME,* corporal,' the sergeant said. 'We have to get in there and do what we're supposed to.'

"The corporal shook his head, 'We have to DO WHAT'S RIGHT.' He asked Sergeant Ben to think back on the feeling last time he'd stuck to a questionable order. 'How did that feel?' the corporal asked.

"Ben breathed out reluctantly. 'Not great.'

"And the corporal asked the sergeant to think forward, to '*CONSIDER HOW HE WOULD WANT TO RE-MEMBER THIS TIME, YEARS FROM NOW.'*

"Mostly the two of them went at it while the rest of us just listened and weighed in from time to time. We talked and talked and with each passing consideration we went DEEPER AND DEEPER into it. We ignored the sound of buzzing mosquitoes, of jungle rain, of every obstacle. There was too much at stake. Nothing could stop us, nothing could interfere with OUR REACHING COMPLETE AND TOTAL AGREE-MENT ON THE BEST WAY TO ACT. We went 'round and 'round. Careers and relationships—and the lives of people we would never know, either way, were at stake.

"Finally, we put it to a vote. Eleven of us nodded to the colonel, raised our hands in agreement."

Chuck's hand, where it lay, relaxed in his lap, suddenly twitched, as if some internal fight was raging inside the big man.

"One of us," Franklin continued, "hadn't raised his hand. The *sergeant* sat there stubbornly re-sisting. But we waited."

For ten minutes Franklin spoke—softly urging, encouraging, his smooth solid tone barely more than a whisper . . .

"Finally, giving a deep sigh, the sergeant woke up and nodded and gave us clearance, *Six-Six-Six-KI*, to get that transport out of the thick, obscuring jungle. To do the right thing. To *turn in, Six-Six-Six-KI, the right direction*. Finally—felt really good about ourselves."

Chuck's hand slowly rose into the air.

"*Remember this . . .* " And Franklin reached out, put a momentary *grip* on Chuck's right collarbone, "That'll be great . . . " he said, voice returning to normality. "When you think we'll *have those papers, our clearance approved.*"

Chuck shook his head. "Ah, wha—?"

"When the *clearance . . .* " Franklin trailed off.

Chuck blinking, trying to clear his . . .

" . . . Chuck, *you'll have approved . . .* "

"Oh, right," Chuck blinked. "Ah—shouldn't take more than five, ten minutes . . . to get into the system . . . " answering with more enthusiasm.

The power of permissive suggestion. The right thing said at the right time. In just the right way. Maybe . . .

"It's full," Franklin said brightly, looking down.

"*Uh*—" Chuck shook his head rapidly side-to-side, followed Franklin's eyes—saw the fat red bag hanging there full.

"*Oh! Sorry!*"

He pulled the needle out of Franklin's arm.

10

The Old Pelican

"UUUUH . . . " Everon grimaced.

Alongside the air museum was the huge beat-up old helicopter, red and white stripes under the dust, an HH-3F, a Coast Guard Pelican.

How long's it been here? He frowned at the thick, barren elm that punched up into the cold night sky between two of its five old rotor blades.

It wasn't all bad. Visibility would be good all the way around the nose of the craft—windows on both sides went all the way to the floor. On either side of the Pelican's bulbous nose were mounted two white wheel pontoons to keep the craft balanced during emergency water landings. Rubber tires protruded below. Mounted above its sliding side cargo door was a powerful hoist.

He slid back the door and dodged a pair of squirrels that shot right at him.

The interior looked even rougher than the outside. Flakes of crud. Gray seats falling apart. Half-eaten acorns. *Sue was right. Doesn't look like it has much chance of flying.*

"Whatchudoin?" a voice called. A saggy-eyed, baggily-dressed old guy wearing a pair of blue coveralls appeared at the door of the museum.

"Do you know anything about this machine?" Everon asked.

"Ah should. Ah'm the owner of this here museum and everything in it including this here helicopter."

"You must be Mr. Gunn."

"Sam." They shook hands.

Everon studied the big machine. "Will it run?"

"Not sure. Been half a year ah guess. Old bird ain't nearly old as me though. Helicopter company only built a hundred an' fifty ah these S-3s an' a movie studio six months ago had 'er outta here, rented 'er offa me for a coupla weeks. Put a lot into 'er, gettin' 'er to fly again. Them General Electric Tuboshaft engines is good ones though. Uscta use 'em in the President's chopper, Marine One's jus' like this one ya know."

Right now Everon didn't want to know. But the old guy rambled on: Sam and his wife had just arrived at the airport—he'd woken up at nine o'clock this evening when he'd thought the bomb's shock wave was his wife rousting him out of bed. "Refused ta let me sleep, worrying about everything under the sun 'til ah couldn't take it no more."

The power was out. Their radio didn't work. But their old car still did. They drove down to the airport to see what was going on. He'd been surprised none of her guesses had been right. She'd never thought of an atom bomb. Neither had he.

"These flyin' boats—used to r'cover A-pollo capsules out of the drink with 'em—Coast Guard ran 'er 'fore ah got 'er."

"Can you rent it—er, *her* to me?" Everon asked, rushing a word in.

"What you gonna do with 'er?"

"We're making an emergency run into the city."

"Hmmm. Well . . . you take 'er, if you think it'll do anybody any good. Wish I could go with you. My feet don't work so well anymore. Ah was in that little police action we did, you know—Vietnam."

The old craft's batteries were shot. The Pelican's fuel had been sitting so long it turned to sludge. From the tower generator locker, John Coates let Everon borrow a portable drill and a few wrenches. But he soon found nobody at the airport would sell him anything.

There were four things Everon couldn't take: Doing a job over again—*do it right the first time!* Being so close to something he could almost touch it but prevented from his desire by some kind of barrier—*barriers are meant to be broken down!* Being right in the middle of a project and having it canceled—*someone reneging on a contract.*

And being told *"No."*

Trying to fly from Teterboro into the city to look for Cyn was turning out to have all four. It was pissing him off.

No's were meant to be turned into *yes's.*

In the middle of the airport's perimeter highway,

he found a stranded diesel tank trucker whose semi wouldn't run and talked him into selling his two spare batteries.

Then he needed fuel.

He thought about trying to carry it in on foot, ten gallons at a time, using two of Sam's old five-gallon jerry cans. The pilot's manual he found under the pilot's seat said the Pelican held six hundred gallons. He wanted to fly with full tanks. *Sixty trips past the military? Not likely.*

Sam loaned him the museum's ancient fuel truck.

"Where are you going?" the guards at the gate asked.

"I've got a line on some fuel if you think the Red Cross or the military can use it," he lied.

They let him through.

He talked the trucker he'd gotten the batteries from into selling him seven hundred gallons of fresh diesel. Another trucker he talked into filling the two jerry cans with gasoline. He headed back in.

"Did you find any fuel?" the guards asked.

"Unfortunately not," Everon shook his head.

He was allowed to bring the old tanker back inside.

Everon drained the Pelican's tanks, and with gasoline in the two jerry cans, he cleaned out the Pelican's fuel lines.

In a rear cabinet he found an old maintenance manual. He lubricated every point listed. Checked the fuse panel, replaced several bad fuses, and reconnected two broken wires. He could feel the clock ticking as he worked. He was burning time. *Cyn's time!*

The transmission looked okay. He'd know better if he got the old bird turning. But before he could even try starting the twin turbines a major problem was still with him—that tall elm, standing between her rotor blades.

They must have rolled the thing in here with the blades collapsed, he figured. Disassembling the main rotor, moving the whole machine out piece-by-piece to some suitable launch spot would take hours he didn't have. *How do I hide that from the military? And that damn Vandersommen's probably around somewhere too.*

He went to Sam.

"Is there any chance I could cut down that elm?"

"That old tree don't look so healthy. Prob'ly elm disease. Guess you'd be doing me a favor. It ain't gonna be easy to get 'er out-a there though."

Everon found a guy in a maintenance hangar with a chainsaw. The guy cranked it up and cut a big V halfway through, then started on the other side of the trunk.

Despite Everon hanging desperately on lower branches along the tree's east side, the elm refused to cooperate. It tilted north until it picked up speed and went over with a sweeping crash, right onto the roof of the museum.

Everon grimaced. *Better than falling onto the chopper.* But he worried. Would that be it? Would Sam call a halt to the entire insane idea he was chasing?

Sam surveyed the crack in the museum's eave, shrugged and said, "No harm done. Get in and give 'er a kick."

Everon climbed inside.

If it ran—no matter what, this time he was going in.

11

Magic Words

Franklin raced back down the hill, concerned he'd gone too far. *I've never done anything like— Not even for people at the church . . .*

He slowed to cross the big intersection at Route 46, then picked up his pace again, head shaking: *never without their permission—someone expressing a personal desire for change—*

Even then it had caused him grief.

Using psychology and hypnosis to help church members solve personal problems had only gotten him a dressing down by Reverend Maples. He could hear the senior minister now:

"Prayer, Franklin. It's the only way!"

And worse still, Franklin thought, *that Red Cross guy'll never come through anyway!*

At the pedestrian gate where he'd left the airport, coiled razor wire now topped the chain-link fence, soldiers in gray urban camouflage now blocked his way. Checking IDs and credentials.

"No entry without proper military authorization," said the soldier to his right, a man with short fuzzy hair and mottled skin like charred coal.

"I came through this same gate only an hour ago," Franklin explained.

"Airport access is severely restricted now. What business do you have at Teterboro?" The man was trying to act tough, but Franklin sensed a friendly warmth underneath.

"I flew in on that jet over there," Franklin pointed to the small white WILLIAMS Lear lined up in the middle of half a dozen other aircraft. Neither Everon nor Andréa was in sight. "I'm a minister. I was up at the hospital trying to organize a Red Cross mission."

A second soldier, a pink-faced serious young man in black plastic glasses, eyeballed Franklin's dark tied-back hair. The jeans, the black leather jacket. "Do you have some kind of church ID that says you're a minister—or something that identifies you with that aircraft?"

Franklin's hand went to his back pants pocket. *Empty!* In all the rush—Everon's call at Ash Cave, getting to the jet, the aborted Robinson flight—he'd left his wallet in his fanny pack with his climbing gear.

"Uh—I left my wallet in the plane."

Another soldier, tough-looking, massive, wearing a slanted dark beret and sergeant stripes, stepped over. His full cheeks and bulging lips looked ready to explode. The name on the uniform said PAGE.

"No ID, no entry!" Page snapped. "Nobody's allowed to fly outta here." Page's was a sickly, psychotic voice.

"Sarge, maybe we ought to let him in," said the first soldier.

"*Shut it!*" Page leaned in, got right in Franklin's face. "Go back up ta the hospital! Plentya sick and dyin' up there for *ministers* ta take care of!"

The soldiers under Page's command seemed perfectly used to his lack of consideration. And Franklin felt no embarrassment. Only determination.

I have to get through!

He was already studying Page, senses collecting data: heart rate, skin tension. *How many friends, how many relatives has this man probably lost in the city? He's just following somebody's orders. It's only the sound of a sick soul trying to push away its pain.* But the man wasn't going to listen to reason. *What can I use—to get past him?*

But then strangely, Franklin suddenly shut down.

What's wrong with me? Doubts creeping in: *I didn't really get anywhere with that hospital guy, did I?* He couldn't think. He couldn't process. Couldn't understand. He glanced at the distant glow on the sky. *I have to get in there! Analyze! Is—is Page falling back on—on his military training? The same way I would—?*

"Move on or be put under arrest!" Page shouted in his face.

Franklin knew how it was. His own Army

training had been fun—once his drill sergeant reported his climbing ability. Right out of boot camp the Army began using him to teach rappelling to Special Forces troops at Cliffside, Colorado . . .

"Okay," Page said. "That's it. Lock him up!"

"But what if he *is* a minister, Sarge?"

"What if I'm the tooth fairy? *You heard me!*"

Franklin's hands shot to the chain-link fence.

Page's men tried to pull him away. *Half-heartedly,* Franklin thought. *They'll have to do better than that!*

Resist!

His hands gripped like steel. *Orders given, orders obeyed! Independent thought replaced by obedience! Just like South America.* The story he'd told Chuck was true, with one fatal exception. They hadn't just flown away. He never did understand why out of all the possible cartel operations to go after, they'd been ordered to target that particular village. And nobody would ever tell him.

The same way Sergeant Page has no clear reason for what he's doing now!

The two men under Page's command struggled harder, trying to rip him from the fence. One lifted his feet. Page's beret went flying as he jumped in too, twisting him one way then back, until his legs were straight out from the gate post. The hip on Page's camo pants caught on a wire in the chain-link fence—*RrriiiiP!* The gray fabric tore.

"What's going on here!" a clipped, sophisticated voice called out. A colonel quickly stepped up

alongside Page. His gray camo field uniform bore no medals or ribbons but its shiny metal plate read: MARSH.

The men dropped Franklin's legs. Sturdy, square-bodied, sandy hair going gray, Marsh seemed a by-the-rules officer. But something about the man said: *FAIR.*

Franklin got his feet beneath him, stood—but this time just inside the fence—while Page explained.

"This man has no ID—claims he came in on a plane over there!" he scoffed angrily. "Trying to scam his way into the airport with some line about a phony Red Cross mission!"

"We can't have that!" Marsh agreed.

Franklin had really pissed the sergeant off. If there was one thing an Army sergeant knew, it was how to handle his senior officers—something Franklin understood even if he hadn't liked. When finally it came time to re-enlist, from an Army base in Texas he'd called the only living person he truly trusted. Cynthia. His sister's advice, simple: *"Don't let your life's right thing pass you by."* Nine years later, Franklin was ordained.

Watching Colonel Marsh now, Sergeant Page, the two men under them, Franklin had a disturbing thought. *Orders given, orders obeyed. Like the demands made by the church's senior minister, Ralph Maples. The religious mind—the military mind. Both dependent on top-down orders—is there some connection? Can this help me get in somehow?* He didn't quite—

"Colonel Marsh! What are you doing?" a new voice roared with the sound of command. The approaching big, bald, bullet-headed officer was a two-star general! The polished metal name tag over the left pocket of his dress dark greens said ANDERS.

"Informing this civilian of the prohibition on unofficial rescues—"

"Snap it up then, Colonel! Officially sanctioned military flights only! I'm due at Newark in twenty minutes. Is there going to be a problem handling this airport, Colonel? Because if there is—"

"Not a problem, sir," Marsh said. "Alright, men!"

They began to peel Franklin's fingers off the fence tubes. He was moments from Page's men hauling him off—without reprieve this time. *These men and their inane orders! Won't let me inside! It's Cynthia's life!* His mind ran furiously, trying to think of any way he could talk himself around them, when a familiar voice in his ear said,

"What's going on?"

It was the big man himself, lugging a large green suitcase, a big red plus-sign on its side. Chuck Farndike smiled at Franklin. "Got everything we need right here."

We? Franklin looked at him silently. *He was supposed to set up Everon's clearance—that's all!*

But Linguistic Reprogramming was about more choices, not less. Probably some of the suggestions had worn off. Not the things Chuck really wanted, though.

"They won't let me back into the airport," Franklin explained.

Franklin got it. Being a blood coordinator was no doubt a valuable service but not up to Chuck's capabilities or true desires, the way he saw himself. To stay there collecting blood, a part of Chuck would have died.

Chuck looked at General Anders, and taking a deep breath, chest swelling, pulled an ID from his right pocket. Head point to Franklin. "This minister is assisting on a registered Red Cross mission to the city," voice suddenly stronger. Official sounding.

Franklin almost smiled. He could breathe again.

"What aircraft?" Sergeant Page asked.

"Six-Six-Six-Kilo-India."

"Is it on the list?" Marsh asked. The sergeant ran a finger down his clipboard.

With narrowed eyes, Anders looked Chuck up and down, the heavy muttonchops, the shabby pale-green hospital scrubs, doubt filling the general's face.

Page's finger stopped halfway down. Frowning. "Here it is. On the new list. Why didn't you say—"

Anders nodded reluctantly. "Okay. Let them in, but let's get a move on, Colonel."

"Sir, I'm concerned we may have located these emergency medical facilities too close."

"I haven't got time to consider that right now."

"But if the wind changes—"

"You have your orders!"

"Yes sir!"

"And get that uniform fixed, Sergeant."

"Uh—yes sir!"

Anders moved off rapidly toward a squared-off old green sedan out of the 60s, a large white star on the door. Marsh looked at the sergeant. "You heard the general. Carry on!"

Page saluted. The colonel rushed off toward the tower.

With a sneer on his face, holding the side of his pants together, Page stepped back from the other soldiers, allowing barely enough room for a man to squeeze through.

Chuck sucked in his gut. He and Franklin pushed between them and hustled for the plane.

12

Victoria's Rising Water

"Where am I?"

A glittering silver pole rose from the floor near her head. There was a dull ache in her left leg, bent strangely at the knee around a second pole—*wasn't I sitting on the other side of it?*

The air felt damp and dusty. Above her head, a long row of lights glowed dimly, highlighted the orange of the seat where she'd been sitting—*what seemed like only moments before.* She could make out enough to remind herself of the last thing she could remember—*I was riding in a subway car!*

What time is it? A couple more minutes we'd have been into 59th and Lex! She brushed something from her eyes to read her watch. Its digital readout was blank. She tried to move. *"Ye-aaahhhhhhhhhhhh!"*

Her vision cleared instantly as overwhelming pain shot up her leg, snapping her to full consciousness. Victoria Hill clamped down on the scream and through gritted teeth, sucked in breaths of damp air—*is my knee broken?* She held a breath and ran fingertips lightly around her kneecap, afraid to try to straighten it again. It was dry. *No blood. Skin's not cut—not yet. Be careful of it!*

The long car was sitting at an angle. People were jumbled around, groaning, someone crying faintly. Victoria touched her right forefinger to a cold area near her right temple and let her breath escape. *Wet, slippery—blood,* she thought.

The blood shocked more than scared her.

She gripped hands around her upper thigh, trying to choke off the next wave pulsing through her knee. The worry, the mind-invading fear of further bone and tissue damage, was reinforced by shooting pain at her slightest movement.

The pain receded. She pulled her jacket collar tighter around her neck. And from the car's end she recognized another sound. The gurgle of water pouring in.

"Come on!" she shook the white-haired man.

His eyes opened and he smiled faintly. There was wet blood matted in his hair. "Hi. My name's Victoria. We've got to move up to the other end. The water's getting higher."

"I know who you are, Miss Hill. I've seen you on TV before."

A dark-skinned man in a baseball cap with *StreetNews!* on the front, and another man who spoke no English, pulled her up, while the transit engineer helped the old man. Arms across their shoulders, she hobbled on her one good leg. The screaming pain rolled up in waves: calf-knee-thigh-pelvis-calf—almost more than she could bear.

They eased her onto one of the plastic seats in the upper third of the car.

"I normally wouldn't do this—" the guy in the green baseball cap muttered, "I have to buy these but—" He pulled out several folded newspapers from a large black bag.

"Ahhhh, thank you," she said as he eased them gently beneath her knee.

"I don't expect to have a lot of customers right now," he said.

She spotted her black purse floating in the dark water. "Look in there, will you? There should be a couple of twenties. My phone too."

But he didn't go for the purse. "That's *okay,* lady," he said, an uncomfortable stress in his voice. And then she realized the half-submerged lump floating nearby was a body, a gas-bloated man in a dark suit.

"We can't just sit here waiting for the water to take us," Victoria told the others. There were six of them. The only other woman was shaking her head, pointing at her cellphone, speaking to the man with her in a language Victoria didn't recognize.

"Someone will come for us soon!" said a portly man with a high, annoying voice.

"But *how soon,* man?" said the newspaper vendor. "Before the water rises over our heads?"

"What about opening the front door by your

compartment up there?" Victoria pointed. "Maybe we can walk up the tunnel. If you—"

The engineer shook his head. "Cave-in, lady. I can't tell how much of the tunnel's blocked that way. My flashlight's dead. We're safer in here."

They turned back to the rising water, already inches higher in the minute or so they'd spent debating.

I wish I could look for myself, she thought. *I need something to bind my knee.* She looked at the newspapers. Her scarf. The lining of her coat. "Does anyone have a knife?"

The newspaper vendor had a knife.

She talked him out of a couple more newspapers from which she rolled tight paper tubes on a diagonal three pages thick. Using them like splints, she tied off four above and below her knee with strips of scarf and coat lining. She probably still couldn't walk on her own, but it did feel better.

Something cold licked Victoria's heel and she jerked her swollen leg away. *Water! Already?* The pain shot right into her pelvis. She gritted her teeth, clamping hands around her thigh again. Not quite as bad. The splints were helping. They'd work for a while. Until they got wet.

She pulled herself up on one of the train's vertical steel hand poles and slowly worked her way to the train's front door. It was locked. She peered through the glass. *The engineer's right. You can't see anything.* She turned to see him watching her. They were all watching her.

"Do you have the key?"

"I don't know if we should—"

"I know we shouldn't!" the high-pitched guy interrupted the engineer.

She held out her hand insistently, waiting, until the transit engineer produced a silver key from his pocket, stepped around her and thrust it into the lock.

The door slid back with a *whooosh!* A breeze flowed. And another sound. Behind them. Water pouring in. Fast. The door had been acting as an airlock. Now there was nothing to hold the water back. And just outside, a wall of dirt.

"Close it! Close it!" the portly man screamed as the transit engineer thrust the door closed and locked it again.

The breeze was gone. But the water in those few moments had risen a good six inches higher up the low end of the car.

"Well I guess we know not to try that again," said the engineer.

"Sorry," she said.

"Don't be sorry," said the old man. "It was a good idea."

"Yeah," said the news vendor. "But how the hell they gonna get us out?"

13

Desperation

At the jet Franklin introduced Chuck to Andréa and began to tell her about the Red Cross clearance. She held up a hand, shaking her head, "I have some bad news for you. I know you guys wanted to go into the city."

"What?" Franklin's breath caught.

"Everon lost the helicopter."

"The one he rented?" Franklin asked.

"The Army took it."

"Damn military just let us in!" Chuck said fiercely. "Doesn't sound like our clearance will do us much good now, does it?"

Franklin's lips silently formed a swear word he didn't use anymore. He stared at the ground. All he could see was Cynthia, Steve, Melissa—trapped beneath burning beams, surrounded by fire that raged like pain, through the veins of his wrists, the tendons of his palms.

"At least I was able to get you back in to your jet," Chuck said. "I'll leave you some iodine drops." As he flicked the latches on his case he spoke to Andréa. "You should both take some right away. Protects the thyroid."

"Hey!" Andréa pointed over Franklin's shoulder. "Look at that!"

Far down the street, in the control tower lights a tree tilted. Its angle slowly increased, picking up speed until it fell behind the tower.

"Wonder what that's about." Chuck said.

A minute later, a young guy in a shaggy green coat ran up carrying a chain saw, checking numbers on aircraft, breath pumping out clouds of white steam. "Who's Franklin Reveal?"

"I am."

He threw a thumb over his shoulder, "Your brother's looking for you. Third building down. He said to tell you: Grab your stuff, and *hurry!*"

Franklin quickly threw the straps to his bags over his shoulders, too rushed to notice that airport security guard Vandersommen was back, watching from the shadows.

☩ ☩

The old Coast Guard bird was as ready as Everon could make it with the tools he had available. He gave the starter a try. No less cranky than its owner, the exhaust ports coughed out blasts of thick black smoke. But he kept at it, turning

the big turbine over and over. He could hear the
starter grinding down as its batteries ran out of
juice.

Hopeless, he thought.

He switched over to engine number two. It
turned over more slowly than the first—

The old engine made a rattling sound, belched
out more of the black stuff and cleared. The big
blades began to turn. Their speed increased. The
old Pelican was running!

With the second engine to draw on, he tried
the first turbine again. This time it spun up
quickly and lit. The rotor turned faster now.
Everon pushed up the RPMs until both engines
smoothed out. He slid a gnarled old headset he'd
found back in the crew compartment over his ears
and from the floor between the seats pulled the
collective arm gently upward with his left hand,
testing the ability of the spinning blades to grab
air. *Nothing!* He cranked on the arm's motorcycle
grip and pulled again. He felt the old rattletrap
lighten until he'd lifted her off a few inches. His
spirits rose with it.

A crackly voice came over his headset. "Helicopter near the museum, this is Teterboro Tower.
We show no clearance granted to any aircraft at
this time." Apparently the old radio was working
too.

"Engine run-up only," Everon answered as he
put the chopper's wheels back on the ground.

The Pelican was giving the impression it might

just take them into the city—*and back.* Now the problem was again to obtain clearance. But one thought filled him: *I'm going in this time whether I get permission or not!*

☥ ☥

It was cold out. The sun was about to rise. Franklin, Chuck and Andréa found Everon inside a big red and white helicopter, its blades already turning.

"What *is* this?" Franklin yelled over the sound of the engine.

"Helicopter, looks like!" Everon yelled back.

"This is Chuck Farndike," Franklin introduced. "He's the regional Red Cross blood coordinator."

"Nothin' like a Slick," Chuck yelled.

"What?" Everon mouthed.

"Troop carrier. No weapons. Called 'em Slicks in the Army—Hogs, Frogs 'n Chunkers all had missiles or heavy weapons. Here!" Chuck untwisted a cap from a bottle and pushed a dropper full of some brown liquid toward Everon's face. "Let me put some of this under your tongue."

Everon eyeballed the overweight guy in muttonchops. "What is it?" he yelled.

"Lugol's Solution. We're goin' in, aren't we? Hospital's nearly out of iodine pills. It'll have to do—protect our thyroids!"

Everon let him put the drops under his tongue.

From his bag, Chuck pulled an old gray box the size of a loaf of bread.

"Radiation counter," Everon acknowledged, surprised. "Good!"

For Chuck's part, he was actually covering up the deep twisting dread running through his gut at the prospect of going into the city, something he hadn't felt since the years he'd last flown on a combat chopper. Diverting his fear by thinking about what he should take, *jabbering on like some young weenie about the Lugol's.*

Then again, some part of him felt more afraid of *chickening out. And* some part really did want to go, something inside that felt totally underused doing those blood donations. It was *this,* had convinced him to go in the first place—not the things this wacky dark-haired minister said to him, whatever they were.

Everon pulled his brother forward by the jacket into the cockpit. "What's with the bullfrog?"

"Would Red Cross authorization help us?" Franklin smiled, his first since getting on the jet.

"He's our way in? How'd you convince him?"

Franklin shrugged. "Tell you about it later. Can you fly this thing?"

"I haven't logged many helicopter hours lately. Nan usually flies our MD-900 jobs. But this is just a more beat-up version of one I flew down in Houston, a personnel transport out to a couple of oil rigs."

"How long?"

"How long what?"

"How long since you've flown *any* helicopter?"

"I flew our MD-900 last year."

"And one of these?"

Everon was busy checking fuses when he said it. "Fifteen years."

Franklin shrugged. *Better than nothing I guess.* He'd never seen an aircraft their older brother couldn't fly.

Franklin took a look through the rear cabinets. Beneath one bench seat he found four thick stainless cables, each terminated in an eyelet. Their other ends were joined by a large hook.

"There's a cargo hook back there!" he told Everon. "Do we need it?"

"Maybe."

Chuck Farndike pulled out a folded pair of huge Red Cross stickers. Shoved his heavy green suitcase under a bench. What they didn't use they could leave in Manhattan.

There's a problem, Franklin realized. He looked at Chuck. "We have to switch the tail number!"

"Damn," Chuck said, "you're *right!* What's the—" he stepped outside, a moment later back in. "Two-Two-Bravo-India. Twenty-Two-Bravo-India," he repeated. "Man, I've got Six-Six-Six-KI on the brain."

Franklin let Chuck take the helicopter's left seat and Everon handed Chuck another old headset. Keeping his eyes on the radio, Franklin spoke in Chuck's ear, softly yet forcefully, gripping Chuck's right collar bone, "Really happy *YOU GOTTA* be able to *GET THAT CLEARANCE!*"

"Right!" Chuck answered. He reached overhead to dial in a frequency and began calling the tower.

Franklin threw his duffel bags under the seat in the crew area. He and Andréa went outside and began applying Chuck's huge Red Cross stickers to either side of the Pelican's fuselage.

When they came back in, Chuck dropped his headset on the seat. "I'm going over and talk to those bozos myself!"

He ran off for the tower.

† ⟂

Did our original clearance get approved because Chuck requested a Red Cross mission, Franklin wondered, *or because somebody knew the Army had already requisitioned Everon's helicopter-from-Hell?*

Andréa climbed in the back of the blasting Pelican with a case of bottled water and a box of energy bars, moved up into the cockpit and pulled the headset away from the left side of Everon's head. "Do you really think they'll let you go in?" she shouted.

"We'll see. You fly the company choppers, don't you? Do you know how to fly a Sea Pelican?"

She eyeballed the ratty old gray-metal cockpit dubiously. "Do *you?*"

"Well enough."

"I've got to stay with the jet and try to contact Mr. Williams."

"I could use a co-pilot."

She shook her head. "This old derelict may not have much performance left in it. You've already got Franklin's big Red Cross guy. If I go with you, it's another survivor you can't bring back."

He frowned and adjusted the throttle, trimming back power as the big engines smoothed out.

"I put a case of water and some snack bars off the Learjet in back." Her eyes looked up at him. "Be careful, will you?"

Everon nodded. "Yeah."

She kissed his lips hard and left.

Hunt would want her to stay with the plane? If he really thought about it he was probably better off without her.

Chuck ran back breathing hard from the control tower and got in.

"Fuck it!" he yelled. "It's in the pipeline. I called the first number in over the hospital-military radio. Now they're giving me a hard time. Trying to reach some general—guy named Anders, military commander appointed by the President to oversee all airspace in the vicinity."

Franklin stared at him. "That was Anders before—at the gate!"

"Shit!" Chuck yelled. "Well, I'm not sitting around all day watching blood drain out of people's arms like I did when the Trade Center went. Felt damned out of touch. I was an Army medic—really happy you boys asked me into the thick of things. We get hassled on the way in, I'll get on the radio, see what I can do. *Waiting* for clearance! What stupid bureaucratic *bullshit* at a time like this!"

Franklin couldn't agree more but rose both eyebrows to Everon. Everon shouted at Chuck, "So we act like we have all the clearances in the world—and hope for the best!"

"Exactly."

"Works for me."

Watching the turbines' temperatures, Everon brought them up to speed. The blades were really womping now.

A female voice came from the tower. "Helicopter at museum. You'll need clearance to lift off. All Teterboro Airport flights are restricted today."

"Sue?"

"Yes?" the voice came back.

"This is Everon, the guy whose radio you're using? The guy who fixed your generator? We already have Red Cross clearance for our old chopper. Apparently there's been some delay switching tail numbers to this one. They haven't sent it over yet."

"Oh. Let me check on that. See if I can speed it up for you."

Franklin looked at his brother. *"She* sounded friendly!"

Everon shrugged. "She knows what we're trying to do."

Chuck tapped him on the shoulder. "Screw the clearance. It'll come through on the way in."

Franklin shrugged. *To hell with waiting,* he mouthed silently.

Clear to fly or not, Everon wasn't going to take

a chance shutting the big Pelican's turbines down. Prepared to feign ignorance on the next radio call, he began to lift off anyway.

Up in the tower, Sue eyeballed Colonel Marsh who was busy talking to his men. She whispered to John, the other controller, so the military wouldn't hear. "We have to stop him. Nobody should go in there!"

"Especially not him, right?" John looked at her sideways. "Jesus Christ, let him go. What if it was *your* sister! Hell, he gave us his radio, fixed our power! For fuck's sake, Sue!"

Flames burning above the city. *It's death to go in there. So maybe his sister* is *in there.* She couldn't admit to John or even to herself the deeper reason. She just didn't want something to happen to that beautiful man.

Her eyes shot to the museum again. *Shit!* In the morning twilight, the helicopter's white pontoons were gapping air above the corner of the museum's roof—*He's lifting that damned old red and white death trap off the ground!*

She glanced at John. *He knows the chopper's rising! He isn't even looking out the window.* He was staring at her. Watching her eyes. She hesitated, unsure what to do. She held her breath . . . and decided, giving only a small nod of her head.

If it was really what that blond-haired man wanted to do, she wouldn't say anything.

An airport security guard ran up, now bending forward breathless. "Colonel!" he gasped. Marsh seemed to remind himself of the man's name from the silver nameplate. VANDERSOMMEN.

"That guy who was up here has another helicopter and is attempting an unlawful flight from the museum!"

Marsh glanced at the two controllers with irritation, and hesitated. An innate sense of fair play held him back, a growing respect. He'd heard about the four-place helicopter the man had rented, the one his men appropriated. The same man who had fixed the airport's generator. *And* re-established communications of a sort. None of it the Army had been able to do. *What if it was my sister!*

"Sir, what about the fuel they're burning?"

"Mmm," Marsh hesitated, breathed out, resigned to the annoying little prick. Held out his hand. "Let me have that radio.

"Sergeant," he transmitted, "take some men around to the museum and stop that helicopter."

☨ ☦

Nose angled downward in the semi-darkness, a team of six soldiers ran beneath them. Sergeant Page—uniform bunched at the hip—didn't look happy.

"And that asshole guard Vandersommen is with them!" Everon shouted.

"Coast Guard helicopter Bravo-India!" came over

the radio. "You have no clearance. Land at once!" Everon recognized the voice of Colonel Marsh.

"You'll have to shoot us down!" Chuck yelled back.

As if they'd heard Chuck, five rifles and a pistol were targeted onto the old Sea Pelican.

"Did they hear that?"

"Nope, Bro. Hadn't keyed the mic."

Everon spun the tail around, jammed the big bird over and banked southeast, expecting bullets to come ripping through the fuselage any second.

A mile later the tension suddenly drained out of him. He felt relieved of the night's frustration. Just to be in motion. *Doing something. Moving.*

He didn't know how far they would make it anyway. Right at takeoff he'd noticed what appeared to be a slow oil leak somewhere in the Pelican's turbine seals, but he braced himself with the old dictum silently: *All helicopters leak.* He didn't have time to fix it right now. Every minute lost was time taken from Cynthia and Steve and Melissa.

No one in the dark houses and towers below seemed aware of their passing. A lone flashing police car moved down one of the side streets. Those able to leave had already left.

Everon scanned the early red horizon, wondering how far they'd get before the military tried something else to stop them.

The City

14

Flying Into Death

High in the distance, a billion gallons of radioactive water vapor glimmered—a giant rising cumulonimbus. Its top had to be more than twenty thousand feet, Everon figured—high enough to be knocked by strong west winds into the familiar anvil head fanning over Long Island.

Not twenty miles south, Everon's dad was buried, and his gaze lingered in that direction as if to catch a glimpse of a graveyard too far to see.

It grew lighter outside as they crossed over the Hudson River, the Pelican's long rotor blades whumping above.

Franklin looked out the left side window to the north. The George Washington Bridge surprised him. The long blue-gray span was still connected and appeared undamaged. Cables still hung below their huge curved support pipes where they were supposed to be.

Franklin pulled a pair of powerful binoculars

from his bag. "Looks like the G.W.'s okay," he yelled, the hopeful sound in his voice rising over the rotor blades. "If the bridge is okay, then maybe—" There were no cars moving over the upper level. A severe jam in the bridge's middle was blocking all traffic.

Everon ignored his own growing suspicions about Cyn. Involuntary moisture on the surface of his eyes, he held his own thoughts tightly corked inside. If he recalled correctly, yesterday would have been Franklin's mother's birthday. His *hope* was the same as Franklin's but he had no time to voice more realistic doubts. He was too busy fighting the Pelican's unfamiliar feel.

Across the Hudson, Everon brought them in low against the leafless black-branched trees of Riverside Park, banked south to follow the Manhattan shore, the West Side Highway.

Franklin watched signs of destruction grow more apparent with every passing block. Black smoke from an occasional building. An abandoned police car, red lights still flashing, locked inside the endless frozen stream of cars that had given up trying to go north.

A working ambulance would have no better luck transporting a heart patient.

An isolated glass-front sliver-building burned. Around garbage and frozen vehicles, groups of people moved northward on foot.

Who could have done a thing like this? Franklin wondered, his thoughts repeatedly interrupted by a horrible image he couldn't block, a burning fifth-floor apartment ten avenues east, sixty streets to the south.

What part of this is Cynthia's?

☦ ☦

The 79th Street Boat Basin had been swept into a violent, soupy mess. Listing sloops, catches and yachts aggregated near the shore. A mast here and there poked above the water, their hulls not visible in the murky muck. Thousands of dead striped bass and bluefish floated on their sides. Hundreds of dead green-and-brown-headed mallards floated among them.

Where did those come from? Everon wondered. "Must have been a large swell when the bomb went off," Chuck yelled in his ear.

The sunken boats reminded Everon of the time Cyn had convinced him to fly the two of them out to do some surfing north of San Diego—just after an ocean storm.

Cyn was a fish. She cut through the gigantic waves running seconds apart as if they were hardly there. Fast as Everon paddled, each time the waves slammed him back toward shore, one after another, until an especially huge swell towered above his head ready to smash him down. And Cyn was suddenly next to him, laughing, yelling—"Hang on!"—she reached over and flipped Everon and his board *upside* down.

Everon clung to the surfboard, air in his cheeks,

eyes closed, waiting . . . ocean crashing around him . . . for the turbulence to pass. It was terrifying. *Hang on,* he told himself . . .

When he came up, he opened his mouth above the water and took in huge gulps of air. And in that moment before the next wave hit, he heard Cyn's joyous laughter. He saw the beauty of it. His sister's method worked. Avoid the turbulence completely.

But Everon turned for shore.

He would never get used to it, never be comfortable with water the way Cyn was. Perhaps some primitive paranoia of drowning would always be there, brought through the ages by the human race. Whatever. He didn't know.

He did know water was not for him. He found no single thing more frightening. He would never again attempt to overcome that dull fear. Never again would he attempt to paddle out beyond the breakers. Even now, flying above it, he could feel the pull, that cold water trying to rip the smooth, hard board from his hands—his only means of regaining the surface. No air.

"The Hudson was never all that clean to begin with," Chuck yelled over Everon's left shoulder.

As they flew south, slowly rising, they saw fewer people walking north. Occasionally, in places where the smoke thinned, bodies lay in the street, on the sidewalk.

Franklin looked down through his binoculars. In the cold morning air, limbs had been frozen into odd positions: An arm out straight. A leg bent to one side. Heads at weird angles on their necks. Eyes open, eyes closed. Papery, crackled-looking skin; slick, black-pooled blood; hair spiked out like icicles.

Franklin wondered, *Why would someone want to destroy everything—universities, engineers, scientists, inventors, businesses? Who hates us so damned much? "Dear God,"* he whispered, *"please save our sister. Please bring Cynthia back to us."*

Soon they were south enough to find no one alive at all. When he couldn't look anymore, Franklin reached back and passed the binoculars to Chuck.

Field glasses against his eyes, Chuck muttered, "Someone's got to find out whatever *bastards* did this—some vast and highly secret organization to catch us off guard like this—"

"A bomb can't leave much evidence!" Everon yelled. "It's all blown up!"

Franklin barely heard Chuck add, "The destruction can only get worse as we get closer to its center."

Franklin took in the side of Everon's face, watching as the same thought hit them both: *How far away from the center was Cynthia?*

"Look at that!" Chuck handed the binoculars back to Franklin and pointed at the old 72nd Street subway house on Broadway. "Water's rising!"

A dark wave flowed up through the subway entrances, black, flooding the street.

"The subways must be full," Chuck added.

"That's not water!" Franklin yelled back.

"What—" Everon dipped the nose. As they came closer, the black tide differentiated into thousands of small dark rodent bodies, running for their lives.

"Rats! Hundreds of thousands of them!" Everon said.

"Leaving a sinking ship," Chuck said. "More than 70 million supposed to live in the city. More rats than people. Way more."

There were children lying in the streets too. A small boy face down in a jacket in the middle of Broadway, his right hand out above his head reaching for a book. Red with big bright letters. Franklin could make out the title—*Dr. Seuss.* Another little girl, maybe ten years old, in her pajamas holding her dead mother's hand.

All to be eaten by the rats.

The helicopter bobbled. Franklin watched his oldest brother at the controls. The beat-up old Sea Pelican seemed to be running well enough—just the idea they could be down there too, walking in that human sewage, among the wreckage, flame and smoke, up to their knees in furry bodies, sharp nips cutting through their jeans—

But the rat-stampede passed them *all* by, leaving the dead untouched in their run for the Hudson River. The herd joined up with a second group, and flowed up onto the West Side Highway onramp heading north.

The tips of Franklin's fingers idled around the pointy triangular base of the very old, small gold cross that hung from a chain underneath his shirt. *People have to be out of their minds to live this way.*

It's a loss of reason. And in the next moment it occurred to him who one of those people was.

Everon looked down at his hands. He was holding the stick in a fiercely unnatural grip. An amateur at the controls. *Can there really be anything left of Cyn's building?* he wondered. *But maybe Franklin is right. Maybe we can find Cyn and Steve and Melissa.*

Or will waves of pain and sadness come crashing down full force? Hell, at least we're not just waiting, sitting by a phone somewhere until someone calls to give us the bad news.

Secretly, some part of him suspected what they really would find. But to know that truth today, they would have to be the ones to find it.

He forced himself to take a long, deep breath . . . another . . . until he could feel the craft again. Then to fly, with grim determination, as fast as the old bird would take them.

15

The Giant's Hand

"We should start east around here." From the helicopter's left front seat Franklin pointed an upright flat hand at the left window. "Toward 59th Street. Cynthia's place should be almost straight over. Maybe we can land at the south end of Central Park?"

Everon began a shallow bank to the left.

Chuck leaned forward between the seats to study the cobalt-blue eyes of the dark-haired man who had pulled him into this. "So I'm getting the idea we're going to look for your sister before we try to save anyone else?"

Franklin turned a hard mouth back on the Red Cross man. "That's right. Do you have anyone here, Chuck?"

"All my relatives moved to Florida five years ago. I was the holdout. Just asking— I'd do the same."

To Everon, it felt good to have only buildings to watch out for—instead of people like Marsh and

Vandersommen. But the rotor blades were getting close. Columbus Circle was dead ahead. He could feel pockets of heat rising.

He glanced at the engine instruments. *Running a bit warm—should go higher okay.* He lifted the collective delicately. The whine of the turbine increased. The Pelican began to climb.

By the way he was crabbing, a light tailwind was still blowing from the west. He looked through the top of the helicopter's front windows and muttered, "High broken clouds. Snow tomorrow . . . "

Out above the radioactive anvil.

"Six hundred feet," Everon called out. "That should be enough, especially if we head across the park." He began to level out. "Nothing's as high as I remember it."

Tops of skyscrapers in big chunks littered the streets.

He glanced at the turbine temperature gauges. The needle had risen a little but appeared stabilized below the red zone. "Hanging in there," he muttered.

A huge *BOOM* answered him, Chuck screaming, "Oh shit!" as the helicopter was pushed backwards, nose tilting high, a huge ball of yellow fire blossoming in the air before them, expanding as if to pull them inside.

Everon yanked up on the collective, maxing the throttle, pulling back the stick, trying to halt their forward path—struggled to keep them from the flames.

As Franklin watched his older brother's deft

touch on the controls try to defy the craft's desire to kill them all, he felt strangely calmer than he knew he should have. And he wondered if indeed they would all three die—Everon, Franklin, Cynthia—today in Manhattan.

The blades overhead whumped still louder, flexing against the strain.

Everon has abilities in so many places, he thought, *things I have no understanding of—solar power, electronics, his ability to fly—his competence in business and in everything he touches.*

The earsplitting whine of the turbines rose higher.

Why can't I do the things Cynthia or Everon know how to do? Why can I never think my way through the air the way Everon can—or do statistical analysis like Cynthia does?

Those processes escaped him. He knew the words, the concepts, even the histories of the sciences involved. But there was some barrier he couldn't get past. Sometimes he wondered if it was self-imposed, something he wouldn't *allow* himself to see. To feel even.

He studied Everon's profile. His brother's arms, jaw flexing as he willed the old helicopter to stay in the air. He could feel the heat of the fire reaching out for them.

Despite Everon's usual fun-loving sarcasm, his brother never had anything darker underneath. *The way you and Cynthia are so good at living in the moment— Not like me, romanticizing the past, philosophizing over some random future that may*

*never come. Worried too much over what I'm making
of my life.*

Somehow you guys always live in the now.

*I wonder what Cynthia is thinking? Is she
trapped somewhere in the apartment with Steve
and Melissa? Is Cynthia even with her family?*

Everon released a huge exhale. Franklin looked
outside. *I guess if I'm worried about being in the
moment, I'm not in the moment now.*

The craft was responding, backing away from
the flame's edge. The broken tops of buildings
dropped below.

⚡

"What is that thing?" Franklin asked as the old
red and white helicopter climbed above the fireball.

"I've seen one before," Everon yelled back.
"With Cyn and Steve, one night, having drinks
on the eighth floor of the Marriott Marquis. Down
Broadway, at 41st Street was this flaming ball of
fire maybe five stories high. The three of us took
a walk after dinner. It was still burning. Roaring
up out of the street. The buildings acting like a
chimney. A cop at the barricades said a major gas
main was broken."

"*Gas* main?" Chuck said, looking back out the
side windows. "This one's a lot more than five stories. "

"Yeah," Everon nodded. "The whole city's underlain with hundreds of 'em and the pressure's on."

The city flattened out before them. Through the

smoke over middle Manhattan, the fire and de-struction, was a vision of Hell on Earth. Building tops appeared bowled over. As if a giant's hand had slewn across them sideways.

"Oh my God!" Chuck gasped. "It's *gone!*"

The top half of what had once been the tallest building in the world, the symbol of the city, was missing. Like dozens of other skyscrapers around it, the Empire State had been cut in half like a broken saguaro cactus, leaving only the nubs of uneven girders sticking up above lower ragged con-crete floors and shell.

The U.S. had weathered all kinds of things—civil war, world war, financial collapse. *Can it weather this? Are we at war now?* Franklin wondered. Some countries rose and fell in a matter of years. The U.S. was unique. Of all the places he'd traveled to, he'd seen no other country founded for the purpose of protecting the individual. Something *that* strong had to corrode first on the inside.

South of 20th Street or so, not even steel frame-works remained. The giant's hand had swept out, destroying everything in its path from somewhere near the bottom tip of Manhattan Island. Until up around 42nd, where a kind of transition zone appeared.

While Times Square was a flaming wreck, just blocks north, less than half were on fire. There was a new pattern. Those close to street corners were gone—but structures in blast-shadows of what had been taller buildings remained standing. But for their missing window glass, some looked completely untouched.

"Crossing one thousand feet," Everon said loudly.

"Look at Broadway," Franklin said. "The blast must have been channeled by the open spaces—"

"Like the avenues were rivers," Chuck said. "The lower end of the city is gone. The damage up here is selective."

"Overpressure decreases with the cube of the distance," Everon yelled.

"Maybe there's a chance that Cynthia—"

"Of course there's a chance," Everon yelled back. "But let's not start painting false pictures like you do on Sundays."

Franklin hung a piercing blue stare on his brother, sucked his lips inward, taking deep breaths. "That way," he pointed. "Straight across the bottom of the park."

Everon softened. "Sorry, Bro."

Bro. He hasn't called me that in a long time and it's the second time today, Franklin realized. He and Everon were step-brothers. *Not bro, but Bro. Like he's trying to connect himself, bond more tightly to the family. He's as upset as I am—*

Cynthia's chances were slim. Franklin knew it. *The likelihood of anyone still alive on the Upper East Side—*he closed his eyes and hallucinated finding Cynthia's building completely blown away—nothing but rubble. He could smell the burning drywall, hear the flames. The hallucination became stronger as he saw in his mind the corpses—his sister, Cynthia's husband and daughter—lying there, sightless eyes staring up at him.

"At least the smoke helps block the sun," Chuck yelled over their shoulders.

Everon nodded back.

Across the far east sky, the poisonous anvil-headed radiation cloud stretched even farther and darker—out across Long Island now where snow and rain were likely to bring death to thousands.

"Hey! Another helicopter!" Chuck pointed.

A Bell Executive flew into view from behind the broken frame of the Empire State. Its doors bore a huge logo, a gold crown. Underneath in three-foot gold letters was a single word: KING.

"Nathan King," Everon said. "He bought the Empire State Building last year."

Before Everon could push the stick over to bank them toward Central Park, out of nowhere an F-18 fighter flashed past their windows. A moment later, a fast-attack Cobra gunship rose to hover along their right side, its single machine cannon targeting the old Sea Pelican.

Beneath the ready emotion, Nathan King's deep coolness was missing, mutated into a profound sorrow mixed with rage. It twisted his jovial features.

"Fuck!" he said softly, shoulders slumped,

watching his city burn from the side window of his private helicopter. "There's nothing left!"

"How is this different?" those who knew him so well—friends, employees, business associates—might have asked. His moods, so volatile—one day intense, the next, wild—*sadness, joy, whatever—it doesn't matter. As long as it entertains! Oh, yeah—and get the hell out of my critical path!*

But anyone could have guessed the answer: *"How often does a man lose everyone he cares about, everything his life is built on—in a flash of light?"* Everything he loved, even his parents, killed during a night he'd been doing business in London.

To confirm their deaths King rushed across the Atlantic, came up here to see for himself. The eight sky-piercing buildings he'd created—his parents' penthouse in one of them—gone.

He straightened. Louder and with a touch of vehemence, asked, "What do we know, John?" John Mayhew, his executive assistant, had lost people too.

"Well, Mr. King, the information we have so far from the military shows two to three hundred kilotons. The blast—"

"No, not that stuff, John. What does the government say? What do our contacts say? *Goddammit! I want to know who did this! Don't you?"*

† ⚡

From the gunship's open side cargo door, a soldier held up a whiteboard penned with thick black numbers. *FREQ 144.44.* A clipped military voice over a megaphone echoed the same thing. *"Go to frequency 144.44! Now!"*

Chuck leaned up between the seats and Everon handed him the microphone. "Looks like you're on deck." Everon dialed the frequency into the helicopter's radio display.

"This is Chuck Farndike with a Red Cross mission out of Teterboro."

The response was immediate. "You have no authorization to be here, Mr. Farndike. All traffic is restricted."

"We're on an emergency Red Cross mission."

"I'm sorry, Mr. Farndike, your tail number's not listed as authorized. You'll have to return to New Jersey."

Everon asked over the radio, "What's the King helicopter doing in here?"

"That is not your concern!" the military pilot responded. "Follow us back across the Hudson. Now, please."

The pilot's tone offered no options.

Franklin held out his hand. "Let me give it a try." Chuck handed over the microphone.

In a smooth calm voice half an octave lower than he usually spoke, Franklin said: "We have on board potassium iodide and other medical supplies. People down there are waiting for our help. Our mission was a last-minute Red Cross addition. Please check with Teterboro and allow us to continue."

"I'm sorry, you'll have to—"

"Let them do what they can," a new voice said. "At least call it in."

"This is an emergency channel. Identify yourself!"

"Nathan King."

The radio went silent.

"King!" Everon said.

Seconds ticked by, both helicopters hovering over 59th Street, fifteen hundred feet in the air.

"The tower people have my backup radio," Everon said. "I fixed their generator too."

"Let's hope your friends in the tower back us up," Franklin nodded.

The radio crackled. "Uh—your flight has been authorized. Non-military personnel are not allowed south of Forty-Second Street. Radiation levels are too high. For your own protection."

"Understood. Thank you," Franklin said.

Everon banked the aircraft left and began descending on a northeasterly course toward Central Park.

16

Cheri And Johnny

As fear gave way to sleep, the pretty Latina woman held her child where they lay on the carpet. Until the dim gray light filtered through the front window. And now Cheri remembered:

Cheri Enriquez's house shook.

"Mommy!"

The roaring wave of pressure had cut off Stevie Wonder on the stereo, singing to the penalties of superstition. Pounded Cheri and her three-year-old Johnny down to the floor. *"Mommy!"* he'd cried again as they held onto each other, rocking together on the carpet, eyes closed—waiting for the scary hurricane sound to pass.

As quickly as it began, the howling noise dropped off until it was replaced by a dead and eerie silence.

For the longest time Cheri had been afraid to move.

She looked at the small boy in her arms. His

eyes stared silently up at her. He was awake now too.

She rose and carried Johnny to look out the front window. The sky over east Brooklyn was so dark she could barely make out the tree-lined street. Something overhead was blotting out the light.

She tried the news. The television screen stared back blankly. She lifted the phone. *Nothing.* She played with the dial on their portable radio. Only static.

Cheri had gone along with her husband Jáime's wishes: "Better to bring Johnny up away from gangs and drugs!" And for three years they had saved every spare dollar for a deposit. Until they were able to move to the mainly Jewish area of southeast Brooklyn. Today she wished they still lived in the old neighborhood. Where she knew everybody. Where she could still go next door to the Gonzalezes or across the street to find out what Francie Lopez knew.

Jáime would know what to do. But Jáime had taken that job working construction with his cousin in California. When he called last night, things were going so well. He was sending money home again. *Oh, why did he have to go? He should be here!*

As she held on, rocking Johnny in her arms, the raw, twisting knot grew in her stomach. A feeling that she would never see Jáime again.

She set Johnny down and got him bundled in

his winter jacket and hat and they went outside into the dim light.

"Look, Mommy, more snow!" Johnny exclaimed happily. It was cold out, and the ground was covered with a light fresh dusting.

Cheri looked around. Something was wrong. *Snow? It looks so dark.*

When she touched a glove to it then touched the white-gray stuff to her face, it wasn't cold. And before she could stop him, her little boy had lifted a finger to his lips.

"No!" she shouted, slapping Johnny's hand away, scared, hugging him to her. "You didn't eat any of that, did you? *Did you, Johnny?"*

17

East Side Horror

"Probably the best place to set down," Franklin said. "Their apartment's only a few blocks over."

Everon dropped down over the debris-filled remains of Central Park's Wollman Ice Rink. *In a few hours,* he thought, *on any normal weekday, happy skaters would begin to fill it.*

Not today. At three hundred feet above the rink, Everon hesitated.

There were not even people running into the open areas to escape the flames and falling concrete here. Just death.

Gushing streams of water flowed upward from somewhere beneath the ground, producing a disgusting mixture of wreckage and bodies. Dead skaters, fewer children—it had been eight o'clock when the bomb went off. Limbs separated from torsos, mixed with trash and sewage, brick and steel girder stirred into a killing soup of vast proportion.

Never before had such common concentrated murder been allowed inside America.

"When the blast hit," Chuck commented, "people were just going out on the town—probably having the time of their lives."

"Cynthia, Steve, Melissa can't be part of that!" Franklin said.

"I wonder how the pigeons made out?" Chuck muttered, looking away. "Especially baby pigeons. I've never seen one. They must hide somewhere, sick and limping in the crannies around buildings. Even an atom bomb couldn't kill all the pigeons in New York City."

Watching the mess flow beneath, the big Red Cross man added, "This is going to affect all of us for a long, long time."

Franklin felt like telling Chuck to just shut up. But he understood. It was the big man's way of dealing with something none of them had ever seen before.

"That area doesn't look too bad," Chuck pointed to an open area of ice rink.

Wet and shiny but mostly clear of debris.

Everon nodded and set up his approach. The ice glared up at him.

They were less than two hundred feet above when Chuck asked, "Did you see— I thought I saw something move." He pointed to the middle of the ice. "Something's running around down there!"

Franklin looked through the binoculars. Several dark-colored seals were huddled together in the middle of the rink, heads moving back and forth.

"Seals."

"Okay," Chuck said, "but what's that?"

Everon pulled up suddenly. "No fucking way we're landing here!"

Two huge polar bears, nearly invisible until the Pelican had dropped low enough to tell them from the ice, had taken down a pair of seals and were ripping the carcasses to shreds.

Franklin swept the binoculars around the outside of the rink. A group of five spotted leopards of some type Franklin didn't recognize padded the rink edge. It was difficult to say whether the leopards were more concerned about the bears or the ice. But they kept their distance. Two of the big cats were ripping at pieces of something. Something that looked like it was covered in cloth or skin.

Everon gained altitude and crabbed east.

read the remaining stylish gold letters. The thin wide sign lay in thick gray dust.

"Looks like the top of the 9 Building was blasted back into the Plaza Hotel behind it," Everon said.

"Chunks of the hotel all the way to the zoo cages?" Chuck said. "That's like four blocks." A terrible darkness rode on the Red Cross man's voice. "What about the Sheep Meadow? That's probably better. Over that way, isn't it?"

"Our sister's place is on the east side," Franklin replied grimly. "Too far. The Sheep Meadow is in the mid-60s on the west side. Cynthia's just north of 59th. Altogether, that would leave us a two-mile walk. With who knows what—animals—*whatever,* in our way."

Addressing Everon, he pointed through the windshield, "Their apartment should be straight east from the bottom of the park."

"I wonder why the damage is so much worse around here," Chuck said.

"I don't know, dammit!" Franklin shouted back. "Go east, Everon."

Everon complied silently, angling the Pelican to the right.

He took them higher to pass over what had been several taller buildings, hovering above an area depressed as if that same giant's palm which destroyed Lower Manhattan leaned in here. But more selectively—smashing only certain buildings, leaving others. Down Fifth Avenue, their top halves were broken off but before they'd crumbled had offered their protection to St. Patrick's. But for a few missing feet of its ornate upper spires, the old cathedral looked untouched.

"The pattern's different here too," Franklin said. "Look how the pressure turned away here, more toward the Upper *West* Side."

Everon gritted his teeth at his brother's unrealistic hopefulness.

They crossed Park Avenue. Far down to their right, Everon recognized the top of the big hotel that spanned the avenue, broken off and sitting amid other rubble in the wide divider.

And around the wreckage, more bodies! In the streets. On the sidewalks. Always the bodies.

Franklin peered through the smoke ahead. A Roosevelt Island Tram car hung slanted by a single wheel, like a child hanging from a clothesline by one finger, stalled within shouting distance of its station. A tickle, a breath of wind, and down it would go. No one looked back through its cracked windows.

He began to feel that same sense of dread he'd felt hanging there under Ash Cave rising inside him; changes in his face, his body's posture. Seeing the trail of death below was like tracking the worst serial killer of all time. *Why,* he wondered, *are there so many stories about biblically-influenced serial killers? What is it those psychopaths aren't supposed to feel about something like this, the average person does?*

"One thing's certain," he whispered, "there'll be a lot to talk about at the church Sunday morning."

� ☩

"Cynthia's apartment should be somewhere over there. Within a two-block radius. About—"

Franklin was pointing right at another ball of flame in the middle of Lexington Avenue. Almost as large as the one that nearly brought them down at Columbus Circle, the big yellow fireball expanded, from the size of a misshapen hot air balloon to something much bigger, completely blocking their view of the building behind and below. Heat rocked the craft.

The balloon shrank back. They tried to see around it.

"I think that's—just off that corner there. It—it doesn't look as though there's anything left," he said dismally. "Hold on!"

"What?" Everon asked, hovering them above a row of converted red and yellow brick five-story walk-ups.

"That file cabinet! On the corner of that building. Right there! It looks like the one Cynthia decorated with those big yellow sunflowers."

"Where?"

"There!" Franklin pointed.

There was so much smoke. Determined, Everon edged in closer.

"Oh—sure as hell does!"

Other than a few partial walls between apartments, the entire floor looked like it had been flattened.

"They keep that file cabinet in Melissa's room!" Franklin said. "Cynthia added those plastic flowers herself to make it fit the nursery. They didn't have a separate office. Only the two bedrooms."

Jagged teeth of red brick jutted upward, part

of the remaining nursery-office wall, acting like a shield against the cabinet's east fire-blasted Lexington Avenue side. The fireball began to expand again. Roiling hot air buffeted the blades hard on the close side, pushing them away.

"Maybe they weren't home," Franklin said as he looked through the binoculars. A two-inch-wide corner of some pink material hung from the front right of the third drawer down, fluttering in the wind caused by the flame. And then a bizarre thought fluttered through his mind. He closed his eyes for a moment. *No!* he mouthed silently, shaking his head.

But the thought wouldn't leave.

"I don't see any place to land around here," Franklin said. "Let me rappel down on top!"

"I can't fly directly over the building with that burning gas right next to it," Everon yelled back. "Too dangerous. That empty lot there would be good. But it's too uneven with all that shit in it. Have to keep the blades level."

Chuck leaned closer to the brothers and cupped a hand, "I thought I saw another open spot—a block up."

"Where?" Everon asked.

"Around the corner of that squat building. Over there—that ten-story on the corner. We can run back from there and take a closer look. Follow that crevasse," Chuck pointed.

"Looks like a collapsed subway," Franklin said.

"Then around that one—" Chuck said.

Everon flew east, over the collapsed center of

the street. "What do we show for radiation?" he shouted.

Chuck held the gray box closer to his face. "Level's between zero-point-one and zero-point-two rads. Less than a chest X-ray an hour."

"Alright."

A block farther on, Everon let the Pelican hover over Chuck's spot. Its middle appeared to have once been a wide fountain. Only the outer rim remained.

"Looks clear," Franklin called out, looking down through the binoculars. "Is it wide enough?"

"It'll do," Everon said. He descended straight down. Light winds had been following them from New Jersey—from the west. Now Everon noticed a change. He no longer had to compensate. There seemed to be no drift at all.

The wind is changing, he thought, picturing the deadly cloud anvilled out over Long Island.

Not good.

To their left a marble statue, a trumpeting angel, looked like it had been blasted from the middle of the fountain into a plate-glass window. He put the Pelican's wheels gently onto the fountain's concrete center and hesitated. He hadn't yet shut the helicopter down. He had no idea if he'd be able to restart it.

He took a deep breath and pulled the mixture back. And the engine fell away.

To the sounds of a burning city.

18

Andréa Tries
To Get Through To Hunt

ᚠ ᛏ

"Another tree, ma'am?" the soldier asked the nurse.

"Oh, that would be a big help. Thank you."

He stood the light tree in the corner of the tent, back from the patients on their gurneys, and extended the pole. He plugged in the cord. The rectangular fixtures mounted either side threw a brilliant glow into every corner.

And they all went *out!*

There were screams and cries around him in the dark. The nurse swore. More yells outside the tent.

The soldier fumbled around until he was able to poke his head out. A breaker had blown. They'd hooked up too many circuits.

ᚠ ᛏ

From the Williams Learjet, Andréa watched the

lights go out, half the glowing makeshift tent-tri-age-city go dark.

Several minutes went by as soldiers scrambled dimly, calling back and forth. Finally the other half of the lights came back on. The military had reached the limit of their generators.

Ꮲ ♱

"Colonel Marsh?"

Marsh looked up from the map he was examining, to the face of an exquisitely beautiful red-haired woman.

"Yes ma'am?" he gulped. Someone had let this woman into the command tent at the base of the airport tower. He'd have to recheck his men's understanding of their orders. *Can't have civilians just wandering around.*

"I don't believe we've been introduced." Her hand turned over his as they shook, a slight feminine bend to her wrist. "I'm Andréa Buer. I fly for Williams Power. Have you got a telephone I can use?"

"I'm very sorry, ma'am, our satellite phones are for military use only. It's hit-and-miss now anyway. This is a command—"

"Even if it's to call Hunt Williams? To get you another generator up here?"

Two minutes later, Andréa's call went through.

"Hello?"

"Mr. Williams, it's Andréa."

"Andréa! Where are you? Are you alright? How's Everon?"

"We're fine. We took off from Kennedy about an hour before the bomb went off. We're back at Teterboro Airport now."

"This is the first call I—I didn't think this sat phone was working, Andréa."

"I'm on a military phone, Mr. Williams. They say it's intermittent. Apparently some of the satellites that were overhead at the time of the blast have moved on around the globe."

"It's horrible down here, Andréa. I've got four million people without power. The whole system is down. Control systems, substations . . . "—the connection faded out—" . . . actually got melted power lines. I don't know how many of our engineers and technicians . . . at that damned New York conference. I'm very relieved to hear your voice."

It sounded like her boss was nearly crying.

"Can you get Everon to the phone?"

"He's gone into the city, Mr. Williams."

"What! Isn't that where the bomb went off?"

"Yes," she grumbled.

"Why the hell did you let him—"

"I don't think anyone can stop Everon Student from doing anything," she said with irritation. "He and his brother went in to see if they can find their sister. Everon was able to get ahold of an old Coast Guard helicopter and they took off about an hour ago on a Red Cross mission. I think they're planning to search on the Upper East Side, a good distance north of the blast site."

The line went silent.

"Mr. Williams? *Sir?*"

"I'm desperate for crew people, Andréa. I need to talk with him as soon as he returns."

"I don't know if I'll have access to this phone later, sir."

"Alright, I'm coming up there. I've got Tally. He can fly me."

"They aren't letting anyone fly anywhere near here without special permission from the military. Um, the Army needs generators though."

The phone went silent again. "Let me speak with someone in charge."

"Hold on." She turned. "Colonel Marsh?" She handed him the phone. "Hunt Williams."

⸸

Hunt Williams finished his satellite phone conversation with Colonel Marsh and stared into the dimly lit Williams Power control room at Juniata. One small gas generator chugged outside.

Every single one of the giant Williams generators was shut down. All of them probably damaged. Thousands of homes and businesses without power, shut down by the bomb's electro-magnetic pulse that had traveled train tracks and power lines out of the New York area. The whole U.S. grid in Hunt's part of Pennsylvania was dead. There wouldn't be any outside power to restart the Williams system.

He had strong reservations about handing one of their only three spare generators over to the military. Until they were able—make that *if* they were able—to restart one of the big Williams coal units, the Williams system was crippled.

The company's problem was personnel. There was only one thing to do.

19

Search For Cynthia

As soon as Everon had the radios, battery and generator switched off, he jumped from the pilot's seat, blades still spinning, and chased after Franklin and Chuck.

The air was filled with a bitter burning smell. Death. He dodged around girders, shards of glass, an endless sea of brick and concrete chunks big as the cars they'd flattened. And always, the bodies.

The Red Cross man was only twenty yards up, kneeling on the cracked, tilted sidewalk to check the pulse of a ten-year-old blond child. A blue leash ran out to one side. The boy had fallen face down next to his mother and their dog, a black lab puppy. The puppy's head protruded from beneath the concrete block that had surely broken its neck. A puddle of dark blood, not quite dry, swept out from the mother's long blonde hair like a red halo.

It looked like they'd been pushed over by tremendous force. He thought he heard Chuck say, *"Nothing!"* as he went by.

If someone was alive here they'd already be gone. Everon could see Franklin far ahead already, bag slung over each shoulder, halfway into the next block of 59th Street. They had to get to Cyn.

Along the south side of Bloomingdale's, smoke was not the only smell. Everon tasted a ragged, putrid stench. It surrounded him, penetrating his sinuses. The morning sun had melted an early dusting of snow, a cold February night turned warm enough to make bodies begin to bloat—warm enough to make hibernating fly eggs hatch, attracted to a feast of scattered carnage. Black specks dotted the humans who were their first meal.

"People finishing their shopping—ready for a glass of wine and whatever," Everon muttered with disgust as Chuck caught up.

"Ready to eat, and being eaten instead," Chuck huffed. "God, that's gross. I hate flies."

Almost to the corner of Lexington, Everon fell backward onto his butt to keep himself from slipping into a long crevasse. The collapsed subway line they'd flown over.

Chuck helped him up. They ran on . . .

There's no real protection anywhere, Franklin thought as he dodged through the war zone that had been Lexington Avenue. Corpses lay strewn among the debris, some burned to raw flesh, hair fried like black steel wool. Others, a completely exposed hand or foot bone—degloving, he'd heard it was called at Hiroshima. Skin and flesh peeled away *like the removal of a glove.*

A two-by-three-foot Mexican oil painting, a Day-Glo Jesus, lay face up in the streaming water, blood-red heart exposed and beating in his open chest.

Every sidewalk tree was broken. *How could Cynthia have lived through this?* he wondered.

But then he saw a single ginkgo, his favorite, most of its prehistoric leaves still on, defiant inside the dark loops of knee-high protective ironwork.

He ran on . . .

Everon gave a wide berth to the flaming gas ball expanding and contracting in the middle of Lexington. The heat was intense.

Most first-floor storefronts were demolished. The remaining buildings had a kind of dark, singed surface. A nail salon, a place that sold sandwich wraps and smoothies were hardly touched. The deli next door, the buildings on its right were collapsed, crushed and filled, pushed in backward by debris. The deli's mangled awning tubes hung out on the sidewalk.

He found Franklin, on the other side of the street, running back toward him, staring upward at Cyn's granite-faced five-story. What had once been a large, attractive entrance was filled with brick and steel—huge chunks of blackened concrete swept into it by the blast.

Chuck caught up, wheezing, bent over. "Any way in?" he shouted over the flaming gas. "It's so hot!"

"Couldn't get into the alley behind," Franklin said. "I tried going around the block—not around the side either. The first-floor windows in front are barred, no way to get through."

"If we had a grinder, dammit! A cutter—" Everon looked up. "Can you scale it, Bro?"

Franklin looked up. He had been studying the building's face for just that reason. The broken fascia certainly offered a wealth of hand and toe-holds. The fireball reached out again. He would be able to count on nothing. He could see the hot bricks breaking loose in his hands. The concrete crumbling.

"Look out!" He pushed Everon and Chuck out of the way. A slab of gray granite the size of a break-fast table shattered in the street.

Franklin shook his head as he looked back up. "Take too long. If I made it."

"If you lived through it," Everon agreed.

"There's *got* to be a way to get me on top somehow." Franklin squinted at his brother. "We didn't *really* try, did we? How long is the hoist cable?" He measured the gas ball visually as it shrank back again. "Maybe when it's like that?" The towering fireball had shrunk to hot air balloon size. It was already expanding.

"There's got to be a few feet on the far corner, somewhere clear from the flame enough where Chuck can lower me down."

Everon nodded slowly, eyeing with trepidation the blazing yellow fire thundering up out of the street.

† †

Boom!

Up ahead, a huge chunk of sandstone rolled into Lexington. "Better stay away from overhangs," Franklin said as they ran the increasingly difficult obstacle course back toward 59th Street. "This part of the city is still falling down."

Everon's eyes followed a trail of smoke drifting toward them from the east. Fifteen minutes ago it had been moving straight up.

"The wind is changing too," he muttered.

They rounded the corner of Bloomingdale's into the narrow entry of 59th again, where the fly-pestered corpse of a gray-haired man lay face up across the sidewalk, his head hanging down over the edge of the subway ditch.

"Ouch!" Chuck said as he stepped around the body, his ankle knocking an eight-inch block of gray concrete to tumble down the side of the pit. It landed with a metallic bang on the partially exposed metal corner of a subway car.

Franklin turned his head and stopped. "Do you hear something?"

The three men listened. The sound of people yelling, and a dull banging from beneath the earth.

"Voices!" Everon said.

"Down there!" Chuck pointed into the ditch.

"Hold on!" Franklin yelled, looking for a place to climb down.

"What about Cyn!" Everon said.

"What if she's down there?"

"She's *not!*" Everon said, puzzled, a little irritated at his step-brother's sudden change of direction.

"We just leave them down there?" Chuck shot back, nodding toward the train. "There could be *hundreds* of people trapped down there."

Franklin looked back toward Cynthia's apartment. "How do we know?" He pointed to a subway sign up the street by a staircase that went down into the ground. "The subway stop is a block from here. Right by her house. We take a few minutes, open a way out for them if we can. They can find their own way off the island."

Everon's lips tightened doubtfully. He looked over the edge. The asphalt was painted with big white block letters: FIRE LANE. "Yeah, no kidding," he muttered.

Franklin turned to the ditch and pulled a large coil of blue and red climber's rope from one of his two blue canvas bags.

Chuck watched Franklin walk quickly along, carefully examining the ditch's edge. "What are you looking for?"

"An entry point."

Everon pointed out a small intersecting collapse in the roadway. "What about that?"

"It's got potential," Franklin agreed.

"How deep would you guess?" Everon asked.

"Fifty-five, sixty feet. Looks pretty unstable."

Everon picked up a dusty yellow brick, hauled back and flung it into the unbroken plate glass in one of Bloomingdale's four brass-framed doors behind them. The window exploded. The door glass to its right was already missing. Now the center bands of polished brass between were clear. "First guy to ever smash a department store window without stealing anything. Can you tie off to that?"

Franklin ran a loop around the door frames, tossing the other end into the pit. The rope uncoiled smoothly, its bulk slamming onto the partially exposed corner of the subway car.

The muffled voices grew louder.

Franklin unzipped one of the duffels. It contained another climbing rope. He uncoiled it too, dropping it into the pit. Then pulled out a shorter ten-foot length. "To tie off the hoist, if say, you were to run back and pull it off the helicopter."

"I guess I can do that," Everon answered reluctantly. He ran for the helicopter.

The pavement's broken edge was jagged. Bloomingdale's was running a sale on bedding. Franklin grabbed a bunch of lime-green dust-covered pillows from the broken display window next to the doors and made a pile of all but one on the subway's edge.

"That should keep it from cutting your rope," Chuck said. "What's that one for?" he asked as Franklin stuffed the last pillow into his jacket.

"You never know—can you keep these here for me 'til the rope's set?"

"Sure." Chuck knelt down and held the pile in place.

From the other canvas bag, Franklin pulled a lightweight rappelling harness sewn together out

f three-inch strips of black webbing. He pulled a
econd harness from his bag and set it aside for
Everon. He pulled on a pair of thin, tan leather
gloves.

"You always wear gloves when you climb?"

"Rappelling only."

Franklin clipped in, feeding rope through the
brake—a big lever attached to his harness. He
leaned back and walked over the edge. The rope
paid out and dug into the stack of pillows.

For the first twenty feet, he was able to simply
walk backward down the crevasse wall, paying out
rope as he went, purposely kicking away chunks of
loose debris so they wouldn't fall on him. The street
was made of layers built up over many years—
slabs of asphalt on top—beneath that, concrete
and rebar.

Farther down were chunks of ancient mortared
stone and brick. Pieces of one type of stone or another tumbled away with every step . . .

✠

Back at the helicopter, Everon brought out the
portable drill. With an attached socket, he began
zipping off the bolts that held the hoist to its supports over the helicopter's side door . . .

☖

At the cliff's twenty-five-foot point, Franklin's feet
landed on a wide iron grate—part of the drainage

system that protruded from a large block of concrete. He kneeled on the grate's rusty brown edge, pulled out the last pillow and balled it underneath his rope at the point where it contacted the grate. He swung his chest over, then hung by one arm.

The remaining thirty feet went easily, a smooth vertical rappel, past dark-brown soil mixed with random-colored tile. His feet made a scraping noise as he touched down.

The dull voices echoed up louder now. The banging vibrated into his feet. He couldn't see but the one shiny metal corner. *The train must be at an angle. Its east end buried in dirt and asphalt, probably sloping downward toward Roosevelt Island and the East River.*

He unhooked and walked across the exposed silver corner, its ridged metal top—away from his landing point in case any loose rock decided to follow him down.

$$\underset{\Delta}{\lambda} \; \dotplus$$

Up above, Everon returned to the ditch lugging the hoist under his left arm, its wires thrown over his right shoulder. He ran over to an abandoned cab, popped the dented hood and used the portable drill to loosen its battery clamps.

As soon as Everon had the hoist tied off, he explained to Chuck how to operate it.

"Okay?" he asked.

Chuck examined the controls. "Pretty simple. Forward. Reverse. No problem."

"How's it look?" Everon called down.

"Feels stable enough," Franklin yelled up. "Come on."

"All right." After laying his rope over another stack of pillows, Everon walked backwards following his brother's path down the cliff.

Franklin knocked on the metal roof. "Hello?"

Faintly: *"We're here! We're here!"*

"Hold on!" Franklin hollered into the earth.

His path predetermined, it took Everon half the time it had taken Franklin to get down.

"How 'bout there?" Everon pointed at a large boulder along what had to be the train's high side.

Together they struggled to push the rock off the car, where it picked up speed and rolled down into the side of the ditch.

"We don't really have time for this shit, you know," Everon said.

"I know."

"Temperature's dropping. The wind could change anytime now, blow the radiation this way."

Franklin unfolded a two-foot army shovel from his belt. After removing a quick few inches of dirt and rubble, they exposed the top of a wide window. A little more digging, its shape and depth became apparent. It was one of the long horizontal ones, split where the upper half could be opened. *Impossible to squeeze through.*

Franklin leaned over the silvery steel and squinted to see inside. And jerked.

A dark-haired woman with huge eyes stared back. A trail of blood ran down the right side of her face. Hit by a sense of recognition, Franklin was almost certain he didn't know her. "We're trying to find a way in!" he yelled through the glass. "Can you open this?"

"It's jammed!" There was pain in her face. Her arms were raised overhead in dark sleeves. *Hanging from something,* he thought.

"How far over is the doorway?"

"The doors won't open," she yelled back.

She turned and he heard the muffled sound of words to someone else he couldn't see. She turned back to face him, "Oh! Yes! Windows—" She looked to Franklin's left. "Seven or eight feet from the end of the car!"

He leaned back and looked along the top. A gargantuan slab of street asphalt covered that whole end. No way he and Everon could move it.

"Blocked!" He moved a finger to the right in a pointing motion. "That way? Doors over there in the middle, aren't there?"

"There's water that way!"

"Can't be helped." He pointed, "It's blocked on this side."

She looked over, then back to him. "About fifteen feet!"

20

The Awful Truth

"Why are we doing this?" Everon asked, hands, triceps straining. "She's not gonna be down there, you know."

"We don't know that!" But it was only his own desperation Franklin heard.

Fifteen feet from the first hole, Franklin and Everon struggled to push over a vertical slab of concrete-bonded asphalt the size of a flat panel television.

As the slab began to move, a breath of air fluttered along the ditch, lifted Everon's wavy blond hair. "That radiation cloud's coming," he grunted. The asphalt's black upper edge went past vertical, rotating as if encased in glue. "Think of a desert storm. Then realize each grain of sand is poison. A poison once inside, your body can't ever get rid of." The slab accelerated as gravity took over until it fell, crashing onto the dirt on the other side of the subway.

Dirt flew as they began a new hole. Franklin knew it. They didn't have to do this. They could stop now. "When she left you at the airport, was she taking a cab—or a train?"

"I left her *in* a cab."

More bricks tossed into the ditch. The train was deeper here. As they dug down, yellow, blue, white tiles were part of the mix.

"What was Cynthia planning to do?"

"Go home to her family, watch TV and go to *bed.*"

They exposed the upper part of a window; its lower edge, buried in the dirt, became visible. Another narrow one they'd overshot. But this one had no horizontal split. *Tight, but possible.*

As they dug out more dirt and debris, the face of a white-haired old man appeared. "Get back!" Franklin yelled at him.

The face in the window disappeared.

Franklin pulled a small rock hammer from his climbing belt and smacked the glass. It didn't break. He hauled back. And smacked the hell out of it. The glass shattered with a loud crash.

He felt a faint breeze from the window as he used the hammer's handle to scrape away shards around the edge. It wouldn't do to rip his skin open on the way in.

With one hand on the climbing rope, he flipped himself around and slid his legs over. As his chest scraped through, he felt hands lightly grip his feet and guide him inside—moving his feet sideways to where his toes found something hard to stand on.

And something cold, too.

☦

Faces stared back at him in his flashlight beam.

Part of him felt like he'd made a terrible mistake, wasting so much time. Cynthia's face was not among them.

The group was smaller than he expected, five men and two women, gathered at the high end of the car, standing, sitting, holding onto silver poles. As if to anchor themselves. Cold was leaking into his climbing shoes. *Water!* Already an inch over the orange plastic seat he stood on.

The odor was strong—salt, and the faint smell of ripe sewage. A swollen male body floated in the water, a man in a soggy dark business suit.

"Are we ever glad to see you, son!" said the man with short white hair Franklin had seen in the window. Blood was smeared across his scalp. He wore an expensive disheveled topcoat and suit. "What happened?" he asked. He bore a calm, kind look on his face. His eyes held wisdom.

Before Franklin could answer, someone else asked, "Where is everybody?" Another voice: *"You're it?"* And then they let loose: "The next car's—We've been here—flooded—Are you—for hours—with the—Train crash?—city . . . "

They have a way out now, a voice inside Franklin said. *Let these people find their own way off Manhattan. Get to the helicopter. Try again for the top of Cynthia's building!*

But he had to tell them: "The City's been bombed."

There were gasps. *"I knew it." "Bombed! What do you mean bombed?" "A bomb!" "Oh my God!" "Bomba! Bomba!"*

"What kind of bomb?" one man's high voice penetrated, a dark damp toupee half off his head. He was nearly screaming. "What kind of bomb could affect us all the way up here if—" the high-pitched sound froze. His eyes went wide. *"Nuclear?"* he did scream.

Franklin gave him a firm look. "We think so. Down by the seaport."

People gasped. The screamer shut up.

In the flashlight's beam Franklin caught two more corpses, a man and a woman floating at the car's end. The woman's dark skirt floated up around her white jacket, their faces already bloated by gas. *Water's about four feet high already,* he judged. *Coming in pretty fast.*

"What about radiation?" asked a guy with piercing black obsidian eyes and skin, a green ball cap, the words *StreetNews!* hand-painted on the front in white.

"Our meter isn't showing a problem so far around here. My brother's on the roof with ropes," Franklin pointed. "We have a helicopter. We can get you out of the city."

"I knew it!" said a very dark-skinned man, shaking his head. He had high cheekbones, a dark, bushy mustache, an orange and white New York Transit vest over a blue shirt. "I was up front in the motor when we came off the tracks. We were nearly into Lex and 59th. Wasn't going that fast."

"You're the engineer?"

"Yes."

"This is everybody?" Franklin disconnected his harness, stepped out of it. "This is the first car?" The cold water had filled his climbing shoes, was rising up his ankles.

"I put the train in service ten minutes before it hit," the engineer answered. "Just an eight car hookup." He pointed down the far end, "I—I couldn't open the door—I have the key—the water . . . " his voice trailed off.

"Got to our car maybe an hour ago," the old man said.

Franklin stepped from one seat to the next, grabbing silver overhead handles for balance.

"You *don't want to LOOK AT THAT!*" the engineer's voice rose in volume as Franklin swung his beam.

Light hit the window at car's end. Franklin jerked involuntarily as a face stared back, sightless open eyes through the tall rectangular glass in the car on the other side.

Halfway up the door, water was leaking through a seal that was holding back a flood. *Everyone in there has to be dead. Probably drowned when the subway tunnel collapsed and flooded. Not long after the bomb went off.*

He flashed the beam downward and perceived ripples in the light, a moving current.

Water coming in from more than one place too.

21

Rising Water

"We have to get out of here now," Franklin said, gritting his teeth as the icy water bit like needles into his calves.

The dark-haired woman he'd seen in the window sat sideways, legs across several seats just out of the water's reach. She appeared to be in pain. Her dark mid-length coat was pulled around her. One of her long, smooth legs was interrupted by what looked like thin tubes of rolled newspaper strapped to her leg's sides, and an obnoxious-looking knee that bulged under the skin.

"How'd you get up to the window?" Franklin asked her.

"I pulled myself up on the bars. Had to."

"Are you able to walk?"

"Not much. My leg feels like it's broken."

He sloshed over, examined her knee. "Dislocated, looks like. There's a man up top who'll know better. I think we can get you out okay."

As she stared up at him, blood matted along the right side of her face, Franklin thought, *She doesn't seem to be bleeding anymore.* He frowned at her vague familiarity. *Probably looks a lot better without that blood in her hair.*

He looked around. "Anybody else hurt?"

"Mr. van Patter," she nodded toward the elderly gentleman, "was unconscious when I woke up."

"I'm alright," van Patter said lightly. "Just a little bump on the noggin. I'll be fine."

"Well *I'm* not fine!" said the man in the soggy toupee. The screamer. "Tyner Kone," he announced. "U.S. Department of Commerce! I want answers! How bad is it up there?"

"No good deed goes unpunished," a voice echoed from above.

Franklin looked up to see his brother's upside-down head wiggle through the now-missing window. Everon winked at the dark-haired young woman. "I wonder if he knows his hairpiece is on crooked?"

She barked out a high laugh.

Franklin understood his brother's strategy. *Keep them from going further into shock.* The water was rising. Everon looked at him as if to say, *Let's get to what we came for!*

"Your attempt at humor is not appropriate, nor appreciated," Kone fumed. He straightened his toupee and pointed. "This water is probably loaded with radiation. How do you propose to get us out of here?" Kone pointed to Everon. "How far is it?"

Everon looked at Franklin. "Chuck and I used

the winch to break out that metal grate. We can take everybody straight up." He wiggled backward and disappeared.

"Alright then. Pull me up!" Kone said. "Let's go!"

Franklin considered the opening—against the bureaucrat's round shape. Despite Everon's ability to wiggle through the small tunnel they'd made, it would be too tight for some of them. For sure Kone wouldn't fit. He wouldn't even make it through the window.

"Yeah, let's go, man! Water's coming up fast!" *StreetNews!* Cap's rising voice was sounding more like Kone's.

"If we try to pull you up through that hole, all we'll succeed in doing is getting you stuck halfway and wind up cutting the rope."

Franklin looked at the dark-haired woman. There was no way to get someone with a bad leg through either. He studied the train car doors and knew what he had to do.

"What's your name?" he asked.

"Victoria."

"All right, Victoria. We have to move you. I need to get everybody to the other side of the car."

"Okay," she said, despite what he suspected was considerable pain.

As much as possible they had to avoid the water. Not because it was cold, but because the bomb had exploded only a few miles away, somewhere downtown near the water. He hadn't brought Chuck's radiation meter with him. *It all depends,* he realized, *on which way the East River is flowing.*

Franklin heard the word again. "Bomba? Bomba?"

A man with sandy-brown hair, his arm around a slim blonde woman in a fur-lined coat bunched around her neck, both in their mid-thirties, had remained silent the whole time. Now they whispered frantically to each other. It seemed they didn't understand what was going on.

"New York bombili," Franklin said—the same thing he'd told the others. The couple looked at each other. "Bomba?" the woman asked, staring at him wide-eyed.

"Bomba! Da! Ya skazal vam!" —*Bomb! Yeah! I told you!* The man looked back to Franklin, who nodded grimly.

"What are they speaking?" Mr. van Patter asked.

"Russian."

"What did he say? What did he say?" Kone asked. But Franklin didn't answer.

The guy in the *StreetNews!* cap said, "Let me give you a hand. Name's Clarence."

Franklin and Clarence carefully slid their arms beneath Victoria's legs. The Russian guy lifted her feet. The dark-haired young woman grimaced as they carried her to a seat on the opposite side. Drew breath sharply as they set her down. It was going to be tough getting her up. *Maybe I can help her feel better,* Franklin thought. *If she's consciously willing to let me do it.*

Ultimately it would have to be her decision.

"If I can reduce your pain before we go up, would you go along with it?"

"What, a pill or something?"

Half her pain's internal, Franklin was certain. *Induced by fear—of what might be wrong with her knee, wondering if it will heal. A second part caused by wondering whether she'll even get out of here.*

"No . . . something mental."

"Uh—I don't know. I guess so."

But Franklin's mind was already tuned in to everything about her—a lightning comparison of her vocal accent and vocal tone—her body posture, even what he could see in the limited light of the dilation of her pupils. The swelling of her full lips, down to the nearly invisible tension in the pores of the smooth skin across her cheeks. All of it poured into him, affected him, and was processed.

Like a well-practiced musician, responding in ways he was barely aware of, Franklin gave himself an inner nod, and in a low insistent voice, whispered in her ear, *"Victoria . . . DEEP INSIDE YOU CAN FALL ASLEEP, REST, ARRIVE AT A DEEPER . . . PLACE TO RELAX, UNWIND, CHILL OUT, VOUS DORMEZ, CALMING . . . "*

She frowned at him. But underneath, she felt her breathing slow . . .

"What are you telling her?" Kone said, voice rising again.

Franklin ignored him. *" . . . DOWN DEEPER TO LOOSEN UP, LIGHTEN UP, USTED DUERME . . . SETTLE DOWN . . . SPAT' . . . FEEL AND SENSE AND EXPERIENCE . . . UNDERGO TO CHANGE AND BE ALLOWING . . . YOU YOURSELF TO JUST LET GO AS . . . YOU . . . CANCEL . . . PAIN."*

She felt a flow of energy through her calves, down into her feet.

Since she had given, at least, her conscious agreement, Franklin was using an ultra-abbreviated form of what he'd used to convince Chuck Farndike to set up their Red Cross clearance. But where he'd helped Chuck amplify his uncomfortableness, he did the opposite with " . . . *VICTORIA . . . RELAXING . . . DEEPER NOW . . .*" Dropping his pitch and volume, his tone deeper still . . .

The third time he said it he looked suddenly away, gently squeezed her shoulder.

What's all that about? she frowned. Then oddly realized she didn't feel so frightened . . . And the throbbing in her knee was diminishing too . . .

Canceling her pain, he knew, *carries a danger of its own: The pain is there for a reason, a warning: Be careful! Something's damaged!*

But now he could do what he had to. The water was pouring in at an alarming rate. Franklin pulled the rock hammer from his harness and stepped to one side of the big window in the other door. He waved a hand and spoke to the Russian couple, who immediately stepped back.

"What's going on?" Kone asked.

"You might want to back up," he told the others.

They all moved back. Except Kone. "What do you think you're doing?" he asked, voice bordering on hysteria.

"Ignore him," van Patter said.

Cowed for some reason by the older gentleman,

Kone obediently stepped over, up on the seats where Victoria and van Patter sat and the others stood.

Franklin hauled the hammer back and smacked the glass. A shuddering split appeared in the window's lower left corner. He swung back to take another swing, but a high rippling sound snaked its way diagonally upward across the window and . . . *SNAP!* Shattered glass exploded into the car. Pieces of tile and gray cement dust poured in, chips of concrete, red bricks laid down a century ago—splashed into the still rising water.

A dirt pile rose fast in the water in the center aisle.

⳨

Within seconds, dirt had risen above the water. Then a foot above and still the pile grew. As they scooped it back to make room for more, struggling to keep up, Franklin began to wonder if he'd miscalculated.

How much can there be?

Clarence, the Russians and the transit engineer pushed bricks and dirt into the water away from the rising mound. More light poked through. Van Patter moved several smaller bricks then wobbled back to a seat, ready to fall over. Victoria used her sleeve to wipe away the small trail of blood that dribbled down his face.

Kone stood on the opposite side seat next to Victoria and watched.

"We didn't know how much stuff was above us," Clarence said as they worked. "We should have tried."

And then it slowed. The dirt had taken space where the water had been. The water was rising even faster now.

More chunks of loose rock rolled down. Franklin could hear Everon digging above. The casual refrain of a familiar tune floated down, Everon's voice off-key, "I've been diggin' on the railroad, all the livelong day . . ."

A couple of people smiled.

Franklin used the short claw of his rock hammer between the door seals and wedged them an inch apart. The Russian guy splashed into the water, grabbed one side of the rubber strip, the engineer's hands above his. Clarence and Franklin slid their fingers onto the opposing side.

Slowly they forced the doors wide open. As more dirt poured in, they shoved it to the sides. The pile rose above the seat bottoms, then even with the water. Hands began to bleed. They kept at it until they had a slot up through the dirt, large enough that even Kone could slide through easily.

They stood on the seats, water to their knees and coming in fast.

"Normally I'd say ladies and injured people first," Franklin rushed now, "But we'll need some muscle up top."

Figuring the Russian guy would want to stay until his lady had gotten clear, he looked at Clarence.

"We'll take Victoria here up next. Can you help my brother, guide her?"

"Okay, okay—let's go!"

"Okay—his name's Everon—tell him I'll give three short tugs when we're ready then take it really slow. Since he's got the grate cleared, you'll want to take her straight up to street level. Do you need the winch to pull you up?"

Clarence glanced at the opening. "No way, man." Like a mole, the *StreetNews!* guy scrambled up through the chute, shooting loose dirt into the water behind. His feet disappeared as if he'd been grabbed from above.

While Franklin tightened a harness strap just below Victoria's gold skirt, the Russian sloshed through the stomach-high water to the doors, lifted his woman up and shoved against the bottoms of her shoes. She surprised them all, darting upward nearly as fast as Clarence. Victoria watched the woman's mobility with something like envy. Embarrassment flashed across her face. *She wishes she could do it herself,* Franklin realized.

When he moved around to her other leg, the strap was already on, the buckle tightened down. He looked up at her.

She shrugged. "It seemed the right way to do it."

She looped an arm around Franklin's neck and the transit engineer helped her across the rising water, around the pile of brick and wet gray dirt to the car's other side. Franklin gave the rope three sharp pulls and its slack was taken up.

Victoria Hill watched the wiry, dark-haired man as he guided her head carefully upward to the hole. Just before the train car's interior dropped away, she saw what the lack of light had hidden. His irises. Electric cobalt blue.

Water rose above the seat backs, touched the lower edge of the train's windows.

Kone coughed and scratched at his nose. For someone in a hurry to go—now Kone didn't want to leave the train car! Making an odd superstitious kind of motion, touching opposite shoulders several times—as if to even himself out somehow. Water halfway up his chest, Franklin ignored it, gave the rope a tug.

Kone halfway up the hole, the engineer looked at Franklin as they strained against the little bureaucrat's bulk. "Feels like the chub's pushing back!" the engineer grunted.

Finally Kone's weight left their hands and his shoes disappeared.

Walter van Patter followed quite quickly, spry for someone so old. The Russian went next. Franklin pushed the engineer up into the hole right on the Russian's heels.

By the time the engineer was up, Franklin's chest was completely submerged in the freezing water. He felt with the toes of his right climbing shoe onto the top corner of the plastic seat back and pushed off to propel himself up into the chute.

The dirt around him was loose, turning to mud. He couldn't get a grip. The mud shifted. He slid backward as he clawed against it. The earth offered no support at all.

The hole's sides were loosening. He could feel the loose gray mud pressing inward on his waist, his shoulders. He scrabbled faster, trying to grab onto something, anything, cupping his hands like scoops.

The mud grew softer, washing backward without any purchase at all. The water was to his neck, closing the hole around him, squeezing his legs, freezing water rising over his chin. He kicked desperately, trying to dig forward with his knees.

His right knee found a sharp object, an embedded brick or something in the muck and he pushed against it. But it sloughed backward. He was going down. Water closed over his chin, his mouth, his nose, his eyes. He could see nothing but a gray milky white.

Even that disappeared in darkness.

22

Losing Franklin

Everon and the Russian pulled the transit engineer from the hole. The portly guy, Kone, was in the second harness, already riding the winch to the street. The old man would go up next, the engineer after him.

Everon glanced at the hole alongside the train. "What's taking so long?" he asked. "How many more are there?"

"The rescue guy's the last," the transit engineer answered.

The hole suddenly filled with water.

Down below, Franklin reached up blindly for anything. There was nothing to grab onto. He couldn't breathe.

He reached again and felt fingers take hold of his right hand—then slip away. He was being sucked down, deeper now, backward into the train.

Something caught the left sleeve of his leather jacket. It was a grip of iron and it shocked him to know who it had to be, to know the water had to be not only over his own head but over his brother's too—startled to remember what Cynthia once told him, how frightened Everon was of having his head submerged.

He slid his other hand onto the hand that pinched his leather sleeve. Another hand reached down attaching itself to his arm. Slowly, he moved upward. But the suction tried to hold him. He was drowning, running out of air.

He was jerked forward—violently!

His head burst clear. He saw Everon's determined face, eyes big, covered with wet gray slime. They both gasped, sucking in huge gulps of the smoky Manhattan air.

The Russian, kneeling down next to Everon, must have been holding Everon's legs for he scrambled forward and pulled at Franklin's arms too, helping Franklin crawl his own legs out of the sucking muck.

Franklin's feet came free and he made his knees, breathing hard. He rose to one foot, bent over, his muddy sleeve taking a swipe across his face, then hugged his brother. "Thanks—*Bro!*" he breathed out.

Everon let out a long exhale. "Nothing better to do today."

"Except find Cynthia."

"Exactly."

† †

Standing in toe-deep water as it rippled over the train car top, Franklin and Everon watched the rope help the Russian rise to the street. The others were already up.

"Climbing out from here would have been impossible for them without the hoist." Franklin looked up. "Nice job getting rid of the metal grate." He turned to Everon. "We can't just ditch them, you know." Rising water sloshed over their boot tops.

"I know." Everon's forehead held a puzzled frown. "That old guy looks familiar."

"Victoria—the dark-haired girl—she called him Mr. van Patter."

"*Walter* van Patter? What the hell? You're kidding!" Everon nodded. "I thought I'd seen him somewhere. That guy's a multibillionaire, Bro. They call him The Runner."

"The Runner? *Him?*"

"Well, he doesn't actually run much. It's a nickname. Did you see those gold and white running shoes he wears? He walks everywhere. Probably the only billionaire in the city who never uses a driver."

The harness was coming down. "How long to get the helicopter started?" Franklin asked.

"Just a few minutes, I hope."

Franklin held the harness out to his brother. "Then get up there and get going."

Everon got his legs in the straps and yelled up. A moment later he began ascending the tunnel wall very slowly. "Looks like the battery's nearly out of juice . . . "

† †

Chuck was handing each person a bottle of water and a snack bar as they reached the street. He pulled out a blanket for Victoria to sit on.

"Dislocated," he said. "Nice job somebody came up with for splints," carefully undoing them. "Franklin?"

"I did it."

"Really!"

When he probed her bulging knee with a gentle fingertip, she barely reacted. "Not bothering you like you'd think it would," he said puzzled, rubbing backs of fingers across red muttonchops. "I can't reduce it by myself though."

The Russian woman said something unintelligible and knelt down behind Victoria's head. She slid her arms to the elbows under Victoria's armpits and said something else to Chuck.

"Do it!" said the Russian man.

"She wants you to try to put it back in," Victoria said.

"Yeah. Okay," Chuck pushed her skirt up a few inches, and with a meaty hand massaged her thigh, pulling on her heel, straightening her leg.

Now the pain came back. Her leg was three-quarters straight when her kneecap popped over and her leg straightened. *"Ahhhh . . . "* Suddenly the world felt a whole lot better.

Chuck replaced the newspaper splints with a clear blow-up plastic cuff. He wound another cloth around her head.

"You should check out Mr. van Patter," she said, as the white-haired man came from the ditch. "I think he had a pretty bad crack."

Chuck used some alcohol on a gauze pad to clean the blood off the side of van Patter's forehead.

"No big deal," the old guy winced.

Chuck peeled open a large flesh-colored adhesive bandage and applied it just below the scalp line. *Probably a concussion,* Chuck thought.

"Who are they?" Victoria asked. "The two guys who got us out of there."

"Who, Franklin and the blond one?" Chuck smiled. "Just met 'em myself. They're brothers."

"Brothers?" van Patter said. "They don't look anything like brothers."

☩

As the hoist walked Everon slowly upward, he wiped sweat from his eyes, more of the gray cement mud from his forehead. The sun was out. *Getting warm. Or is it that gas blasting up out of the street?*

As soon as he made the edge, he immediately got out of the harness and signaled the train engineer to send it back down for Franklin.

The smell seemed worse than before. Everon looked down 59th. "The military's been here? HAZMAT people?" he asked, frowning.

Chuck shook his head, "Not yet." The others agreed. A low hum permeated the air.

"Those body bags," Everon pointed out two, a hundred feet up the sidewalk.

The Russian woman watched where he was pointing. She began speaking rapidly, hands suddenly animated. Her agitation spread to the Russian male.

"What are they saying?" Kone asked.

"I don't know. You can ask Franklin when he gets up here," Everon said. "Something about body bags. I've got to—"

"Look kinda rough," Clarence frowned at the two nearest ones. "Uneven, somehow, aren't they?"

"Oh my God!" Victoria said.

"That's no rubberized plastic," Chuck snarled. "Flies. Thousands of 'em."

"Shit!" Everon said.

"I *hate* flies," Chuck said. "Nothing—*nothing* will ever kill all the flies and roaches in New York City."

Why can't the big guy just shut up? Everon thought. *Rats, pigeons, cockroaches, he's okay with. Flies, he has a problem—*

The train engineer flipped the lever to put the hoist in gear. Everon watched the hoist grinding Franklin upward. Wind gusted along the street. Buildings blocked any sense of direction. Everon could see some blue sky, a puffy cumulus overhead. "As soon as my brother's up I'm going to run ahead, start the helicopter . . . "

☦

Franklin was only up six feet when the hoist
rrrrr-ed to a stop. *"Not my day!"* The cable rope
slowly paid out and set him back in the shin-high
water . . .

☦ ☦

"Pull him up!" van Patter urged. *"Pull him up!"*

Everyone but Victoria, van Patter and Kone
grabbed onto the winch cable. Too slick and
smooth. There was nothing to grip.

"I'll get another battery!" Everon yelled, grabbing
the drill and heading for the nearest abandoned
car.

Everon had the hood raised and was discon-
necting the battery's second lead, when a shout
went up. *"There!"* Franklin's head appeared at the
top of the rope, tied around Bloomingdale's front
doors. Bent over, straining, he rose out of the ditch
hand-over-hand.

Franklin's climbing shoes had no laces.

"Ahh," Everon smiled, running back. "The old
pull yourself up by your shoelaces trick!"

Franklin's laces were wound around the rope,
ends tied in knots to form loops. Slide one up.
Stand on the other. He pulled himself over the
street's edge—to the waiting grip of Clarence, the
Russian guy and the train engineer.

"Faster than changing batteries," he said as he
undid the knots and threaded the laces back in
his shoes. He looked at Everon. "Haven't you got a
helicopter to start?"

"Right!" Everon scooped up the hoist, tugged on Clarence's jacket. "Come on! Give me a hand!" And they ran down 59th Street.

Victoria looked at Franklin's pants, jacket—his face and dark hair were caked with gray mud. "What *happened?*"

"New York's streets are underlain with dozens of creeks and streams," the voice of white-haired van Patter answered for him. "But I wouldn't doubt the water coming into the train is part of the East River."

Franklin glanced back over the edge, rapidly coiling purple rope around a hand and elbow. The rubble above the train was completely submerged now.

"I didn't pay to get on. Maybe the Transit Authority didn't want to let me go."

23

To The Chopper

"Just a little higher, Clarence . . . wiggle it a little . . . "

The newspaper guy cradled the winch in place as Everon reattached it to its tubular support arms above the Pelican's cargo door. Everon hated having to take time now, not being too certain how difficult the helicopter would be to restart. But they would need the hoist to have any chance of getting Franklin on top of Cyn's building.

"Damn!" Clarence said as the green cap blew from his head. "Getting windy." Dark kinky hair stood out in all directions, flipped back in the gusts. *From the southeast now,* Everon saw. *From the cloud.*

"How big was the bomb?" Clarence asked.

"I don't know."

Way down the avenue, thick dark slanting wisps of death, the radiation cloud and its rain were definitely moving in their direction.

"There!" Everon said, *"Got it!"* sliding the last bolt home. *Zzzzt!* He quickly tightened down a nut and moved to another.

Zzzzt! Zzzzt! He moved to the last nut, part of him wishing they hadn't taken time to get these people out. *Zzzzt! What if Franklin's right and Cyn's up there half alive?*

"My mother's in Brooklyn," Clarence interrupted worriedly. "Do you know anything about Brooklyn . . . "

They were hustling at a pretty good clip, dodging chunks of debris, smashed furniture, fly-covered corpses. But the wind was gusting now, back and forth along 59th. They'd left the battery behind. Cars were everywhere. They could always get another.

Victoria Hill rode on Franklin and the train engineer's interlocked hands. The Russian couple, who called themselves Petre and Kat, Franklin learned, carried his larger bags. Tyner Kone trailed the others. He'd refused to carry anything.

The slightly built Walter van Patter carried the small blue bag with Franklin's climbing harnesses. "Has the President said anything yet?"

"Communications are down everywhere," Chuck huffed as he lugged his med case.

"I doubt any television stations are operating," Franklin said. "Only one radio station was on the air when we flew out of Teterboro. Everon can tell you more about electronic damage."

"My family's in the Bronx," the transit engineer rasped out. He was tiring now, his side of Victoria lagging up and down with every step. "Have you heard anything about the Bronx?"

Franklin shook his head.

They were halfway up the block when the transit engineer asked, "Can we stop to rest? Just for a minute?"

An explosion rumbled ten yards behind them. A chunk of concrete slammed into the street, putting an end to the engineer's rest idea. They pushed on. Past where the subway cave-in ended they were able to hustle still faster more in the center of the street.

Victoria studied the dark-haired man carrying her, pushing them all to go faster. Her knee was almost numb. *How did he do it? And he speaks Russian? They don't look much like brothers. The other one—Everon?— the wavy sun-blond hair. Certainly dresses well—* Beneath the mud, she'd recognized quality in the cotton diagonal running through his sturdy tan trousers—*gabardine.*

But it was this one, *Franklin,* carrying her, almost running along the street. The gray mud streaked on his black leather jacket, on his long, dark tied-back hair and face. *Tall and rangy.* A flutter in her stomach. Those shining cobalt-blue eyes seemed to see her as she had never been seen before.

"So you're on a Red Cross mission?" she asked.

"No," he huffed. "We just came in to find our sister."

"She was on the subway?"

"We don't know where she is."

"Does anyone know who did this?"

"No one seems to."

Despite a minor case of numb-butt, she could feel his fingers below her thighs, long and strong. She'd noticed a little dirt caked around their tips. *From where he must have been clawing his way out of that hole.* But his nails were clipped close. Barely any white showing at the ends.

Why the hell am I thinking about his nails?

She felt her face redden with embarrassment. She knew why. *What am I doing? It's only a you-saved-my-life attraction.*

She remembered reading somewhere that more babies were conceived around a major disaster than any other time. *What is it about disaster that makes people think about sex?*

The helicopter came into view, blades already turning.

"We're almost there," Franklin urged. "Come on!"

Cynthia has to be alive! Has to be! A kind of mantra he repeated with each step, clinging to uncertainty, holding tight to his fear. Grief, sadness—they meant his sister was already gone.

Fear was better. As long as he was afraid, Cynthia had to be alive.

24

Hopeless

As they rose above ruined streets and broken buildings, the survivors learned in silent fear what the city had become. Franklin wished he could have distracted them from what lay below, keep them from going into a state of shock. There just wasn't time.

"Chuck, can you handle the hoist?" he asked.

"Of course."

Franklin stepped to the rear of the Sea Pelican's cargo area and pulled a climbing harness out of his blue bag.

"What are you doing?" Tyner Kone asked, voice rising.

"Before we can get you to Teterboro, we have to make a stop," Franklin said.

"Stop? You can *kiss my ass!"* Kone yelled.

"Our sister, her husband and child live two blocks over. The first floor was blocked when we tried to get inside their apartment building. We were on our way to get the helicopter to do a flyover when we knocked a piece of concrete down onto your train."

"These people belong in a hospital!" Kone said.

Victoria gave the barrel-bodied little bureaucrat a severe look.

"Maybe we should just give these men the time they need to do what they came to do. If it weren't for them we'd still be in that damn train. Probably dead."

"I agree," added Mr. van Patter. He looked toward the empty bench. "This helicopter's not full, and none of us are in worse shape than this young lady here. If she can wait, I think *you* can, Mr. Kone. If we can locate any more survivors, we ought to do it."

"Yeah, man, just shut up," said Clarence the newspaper vendor.

The Russians said nothing. The transit engineer gave a small nod of agreement.

Kone shut up.

Victoria sat on the fabric cot-seat looking at him silently. Though her knee was swollen nearly twice its normal size, the pain wasn't that bad.

If I hadn't gone out to the television studio in Queens, I'd probably be dead now. Like David, the guy she'd had a first date with last night. David lived in Chelsea. South. She could see nothing but fire in that direction.

What if I'd stayed at David's last night like he wanted me to?

There was probably still a job here—of some

kind. If she wanted it. She didn't. She didn't want
Atlanta either. So then, *back to Chicago* it would
have to be, she figured.

The helicopter rocked violently as Everon
crabbed them over the wrecked building tops.

"That one!" Franklin said.

There on the floor of Cynthia's apartment was
the flower-covered four-drawer file cabinet, situ-
ated up against that half-broken bit of outside wall.
Again Franklin noticed the fluttering splash of pink
along the cabinet's side.

Everon dodged them around the roaring yellow
ball of flame as it expanded again in the middle of
Lexington. "I—I just can't do it," he yelled. "I can't
get you over top and still keep the blades out of
the fire!"

Franklin studied the building through the ball
of yellow as they slowly drifted around it. *Something. We aren't seeing something. Has to be a way
down there.*

The flame shrank. Everon inched closer. Expanded again. They could feel the heat from it as it
rocked the big Pelican.

But after two more complete circles, there just
wasn't. Not one debris-covered square foot. To put
the winch's hang point over any part of what was
left of the upper floors would put the blades right
in the flame.

At the fireball's smallest, just as it began to expand, they got a brief look at the apartment floor.
The broken walls. Junk littered everywhere.

Fortunately one person wasn't looking down.

"Uh—I think we *better GET OUT—OF—HERE!*" Clarence shouted. *"SHIT!"*

Franklin's eyes shot upward. Pieces of steel I-beam fell past the blades. Furniture and stone work. A statue of some kind.

"That tower's coming down!" The helicopter lurched as Everon jerked them away.

"Alright, that's it now!" said Kone.

The city was still falling apart.

Franklin watched through the helicopter window—pieces of someone else's life falling into the alley behind Cynthia's building.

There was no movement down there. No one could have survived.

With a terrible reluctance, Everon turned off. Banked west.

25

Giving Up

Franklin's climbing harness lay abandoned on the floor.

"It's over. She's gone." Everon's face stayed straight ahead, talking loudly at the windshield, "We tried, Bro."

Ten survivors turned away from the Manhattan shore, and the Sea Pelican's windows were filled by the rusty-green of the Hudson River, on their right the blue-gray span of the George Washington Bridge. In the narrow track of blue between the pilots' seats, the morning sky swarmed thick with giant insects—helicopters of every size and color heading toward Manhattan to rescue whoever they could find.

Franklin got off his knees between the front seats. Left his brother to handle the Sea Pelican's controls. Moved back to take a space at the forward end of the passenger compartment's long side-bench.

"Chopping off body parts one at a time is too good for whoever did this to us . . . " Chuck shouted over the Pelican's whomping roar. Franklin let the big man rant. Soon they'd be back at Teterboro.

Not finding Cynthia filled Franklin with a lowness he'd never felt before. Not the Army. Not the church. He felt like crying—if it would do any good. He couldn't admit to himself what Everon had already accepted: *Cynthia and Steve and Melissa. They have to be dead.*

But his inner eye kept seeing Cynthia's building. The debris. The walls. The alley behind. There just wasn't any way down there.

On the long seat next to Franklin, the pain of the dark-haired woman, Victoria, seemed to have diminished to a level she was able to handle. Next to her, Walter van Patter's head bandage had bled through. Chuck was replacing it.

Franklin listened as the MTA transit engineer debated quietly with Clarence over where the bomb must have come from.

Franklin studied the Russians on the opposite bench seat along the helicopter's right side. The Russian man, Petre, was holding his wife, Kat. *Could it be? The Russians? Or maybe some Al Qaeda-ISIS-Muslim group, like the extremists who brought down the World Trade Center?*

Who cares! Franklin thought.

Tyner Kone was the only loud one. *"How long 'til we get back? Can't this thing go any faster?"*—and was still at it now crossing the river. Chuck looked like he wanted to lean over, open the door and shove the little bureaucrat out.

Franklin ignored Kone, staring 'til his eyes went out of focus. Something was gone now. Something he knew could never be replaced. He thought of stories he'd heard on the physical weight of the soul, a body losing as much as a pound when it left, and wondered, *Do Cynthia's and Steve's bodies weigh any less now than they had alive? Does their little daughter Melissa's?*

But he knew their physical weight wasn't the thing that was missing. Franklin and Everon had always been somewhat isolated from each other. Cynthia had been their link. Phone calls. News updates, passing information. Now that link was broken. Gone.

What kind of a person would do a hellish thing like this?

Everon was right. They would never find out. *Like a missing soul, the bomb's gone. What's left after an explosion to tell anybody anything about who's behind it?*

His thoughts were jerked away by a swift movement between two cumulus clouds, a glint of reflected sun outside the helicopter's left windows.

"Fighter jet!" Chuck called out. "Probably protection from more attacks."

"I don't know how much good that's going to do anybody now," the transit engineer said.

They watched the tiny jet disappear, then reappear on the helicopter's right, over the George Washington Bridge.

"What's that?" Victoria pointed.

"What?" Franklin said, not really paying attention.

"Right there. *There! There—it goes again!*"

"Somebody dumping stuff off the G.W.," Clarence said.

Franklin's eyes focused suddenly. "No they aren't! Those are bodies! Those are people falling off the bridge!"

26

Death On The Blue-Gray Span

As Everon angled the chopper more northward, a long arc of blue-gray pipe, vertical strings of cable, filled the windows. Franklin could see people getting through on the lower level, making their way around stalled cars.

But on the upper deck, two 18-wheelers jackknifed butt-to-butt on a diagonal across the bridge formed a giant barrier, blocking all eight lanes. A third 18-wheeler, a FedEx rig, lay on its side, pinning the cab of the long silver container truck against a big commercial dumper at the north side of the bridge. Franklin could make out a Volkswagen Bug, its top hacked clear off, crammed beneath the orange semi's chassis.

People here and there were struggling to squeeze through narrow spaces. One woman popped out like shot from a cannon. There was blood on her face as she fell limply to the roadway. Those next to escape ran right over her. Like sports fans pushing out a single arena door, they were being compressed in a smashing mass crushing in on itself. But the pileup was acting like a funnel, sweeping the mob toward a wide hole something had broken in the bridge's south side.

"There go two more!" Chuck cried out.

Pressure on the upper deck looked brutal. Tens of thousands crammed against its sides into a space meant to hold eight lanes of traffic. Like the city's rats, thousands had made their way uptown on foot, expecting to escape across the blue-gray span.

A long dark overcoat cocooned around a man who had fallen through the hole. Franklin could almost feel the scream from the man's O-shaped mouth, red power-tie flapping alongside eyes huge with fear. *If he hits flat-footed, it'll drive the bones of his neck right up through his brain.*

Then a woman. She could have had no idea where she was. Long legs, dark high-heels, white underwear high up on her waist, the blue fabric of her long skirt billowing about her head as she plummeted to the water below.

A single fire boat raced to pick up bodies—*people probably dead when they hit the water,* Franklin thought. *At that speed it has to be hard as concrete. Even if they survive the fall, it's freezing. Cold's going to penetrate in seconds.* "Closer!" he shouted to Everon.

"Must be two hundred thousand people up there!" Chuck shouted back.

"More!" yelled the train engineer.

"The whole north end of Manhattan is trying to get out over the bridge!" Clarence yelled.

"Cynthia and Steve. There's a chance they're on the bridge too," Franklin shouted.

"Not much of one," Everon shouted back.

"Why not?"

"Think about the way their building looked. Their apartment. Think about what time it was when the bomb went off. What do you think they were doing at eight o'clock at night? Out for a stroll with Melissa?"

Still, the slimmest of chances, Franklin thought.

"They're being crushed to death," Victoria shouted, leaning her face against the window.

"Transference of pressure," Everon said loudly over his left shoulder. "People in back are only pushing a little. By the time it gets up front, the pressure becomes enormous."

In slow motion, another section of large-diameter railing pipe bent outward to leave an even wider gap, where the monstrous mob launched more bodies into space.

"It'll take days to get tow trucks in there," Walter van Patter rasped.

Clarence shook his head. "Those semis ain't going nowhere!"

It was getting worse. While they watched, people began falling by twos and threes.

Everon came to a dead hover, halfway between the two mid-span lattice towers, where the bridge's main support pipeage curved down to the tops of the wrecked 18-wheelers—while half a dozen more people launched off the south side.

"What's he doing?" Kone yelled. Everyone ignored him.

"Think we could enlarge that small opening between the wrecks?" Franklin said. "Use the big hook?"

"Someone would have to go down there and hook one of the semis up," Chuck said.

"No! It's too dangerous!" Kone screamed. "Let someone else do it! You've got to get us to a hospital!"

"What happens if we land back at Teterboro and the Army won't let us take off again?" Everon yelled back.

"All of us might know somebody in there," the transit engineer said.

"Can this machine handle the load?" van Patter asked.

"I think so," Everon yelled.

"They'll have to wait!" Kone said.

"We can't just leave them!" Victoria shot back.

"Da! Da!" Petre and Kat pointed frantically out the right side window, urging someone do something as more were ejected from the bridge.

"I demand you get us to New Jersey! Now!" Kone shouted.

While they argued, a dozen more fell to their deaths, dropping through the hole in the bridge's side. Part of Franklin felt like agreeing with Kone.

Cynthia and her family will never be found. What's the point? But another desperate voice inside wasn't ready to give up. Not yet. A voice that said: *Maybe they're on the bridge!*

Walter van Patter squinted at the chubby little bureaucrat. "You know, Mr. Kone, some of the most powerful people in the world are probably trapped on that bridge."

☨ ☨

Kone shut up.

Franklin shuffled bent over, to keep from hitting his head, into the back of the passenger compartment. On the helicopter's rear wall, he flipped out a handle and opened a three-foot-square door. He dragged the heavy cable harness across the floor, until its big curved hook caught under one of the seat supports. Petre freed the hook, and with the transit engineer, they pushed the heavy tangle to the side door.

Franklin bent down between the front cockpit seats where he could speak with Everon. "I have to get the heavy-lift harness connected underneath."

"Okay," Everon nodded, gingerly handling the controls.

"The hook says it's rated for six thousand pounds," Franklin said. "Is that enough?"

"Maybe for one end of a trailer if we can find an empty one. Which one do you want to try?"

"Hold on."

Franklin backed up to where Chuck waited. Together they slid back the big square door. Cold air poured in.

Clearly, there wouldn't be much chance they could even slide one of the truck cabs out of the way. The engines alone probably weighed several tons. Of the jack-knifed trailers still on their wheels, the orange one had no cab. *Must have gone over the side through the hole.*

He moved back to the cockpit.

"Forget the FedEx. It's on its side *and* it's probably full. Let's try the orange trailer, the one with no cab in the inbound lanes. It's only got that VW jammed under it."

"Makes sense. Tell Chuck that's the one and he can— *WHOA!*" Everon's left hand yanked upward on the collective arm as a sudden gust tried to drop them into the bridge cabling. He moved the cyclic stick before his knees with quick, jerky movements until the big bird steadied out twenty feet higher. "I'm going to—*hold on!*"

He pushed several overhead switches. Immediately the whole ride smoothed out. "It works!"

He glanced at Franklin. "Auto-stabilizer. I was afraid to try it." He let out a deep breath. "That will make it easier. Okay, Bro. Too bad we don't have all the communications stuff working. Signal to Chuck. He can tell me which way you want me as he lowers you down."

"All we need is to slide the back end of one trailer away from the other, right?" Franklin yelled in his brother's ear. "Those containers—are they locked on their chassis?" Half the trailers on the roads these days were actually a separate container box that sat on an 18-wheeler chassis.

Everon's eyes searched his memory. "Not necessarily," he nodded. "Once we're hooked on, I won't raise it too high. Otherwise we could pull the box right off the truck bed!"

"Okay!"

Franklin backed up. Picked up the climbing harness where he'd left it on the floor. Slid his legs in and buckled its upper straps across his chest. Chuck clipped the loop on the front of the harness to the hoist carabiner.

Franklin showed Chuck the orange container truck he wanted to try. But first they had to get the cable harness attached to the helicopter while still in the air.

† †

Franklin took one of the heavy cable eyelets in his right hand, gripped the overhead hoist bracket tubes with his left and lowered his weight onto the hoist cable. He hadn't known what to expect until he swung through the open door. Freezing rotor wind blasted his hair.

"Okay!" he yelled.

Chuck held the hoist's DOWN button until he was two feet below the Pelican's body. Water ran from Franklin's eyes. He could barely see.

With the bulk of the heavy cable harness still inside the door, Franklin pulled himself underneath, around the right streamlined wheel pontoon.

"More slack!" he waved.

Chuck dropped him down another two feet.

Mounted to the underside of the Pelican's airframe were four metal hooks, arranged in a rectangle. Using his legs he pushed himself into a position nearly horizontal, and reached out for the closest hook with a cable eyelet.

Chuck's head appeared over the door edge.

"A little more!" Franklin yelled.

The cable dropped him another foot. He pushed with his legs and the first eyelet clipped into place. Chuck lay on his stomach and handed him another. The next two snapped easily into their hooks. The last one would be a stretch, way out to the helicopter's far corner.

He strained against the hoist cable, swinging his arm and missed. His feet slipped off the sponson and his weight fell straight down jerking him onto the cable.

He got hold of the fourth eyelet, scrambled using his legs to push himself back up into position. He pointed his toes. Hand reaching out, lunging away from the wheel sponson, the eyelet scraped next to the hook. He fell away swinging back and forth in the violent wind again, not knowing if he had the strength to try again.

But the cable was gone. It was hanging from the fourth hook.

He wiped the back of a gloved hand against his

orehead, as Chuck shoved the rest of the heavy
harness over the door edge and its cables untan-
gled. The big hook squared into position, dangling
twenty feet below.

Franklin nodded. Chuck disappeared.

The helicopter began moving sideways to a spot
above the rear of the cab-less orange semi-trailer
that took up most of the four inbound lanes.

Inside, Everon yelled to Chuck, "How's that?"

"Five feet to the rear. Okay—perfect! Hold it."

Franklin saw Chuck reappear at the doorway
edge. Franklin gave him a downward point. A moment later, Franklin felt himself descend.

His feet contacted the top of the orange container with a clang. Below him on the crowded
bridge deck, rotor-blade blast was whipping people's hair, their clothes. Faces screamed up at him,
people shaking fists in the air, flipping the middle
finger. He had to focus.

More hoist cable came down, giving him room
to maneuver.

Chuck's head appeared. Franklin waved the
hook lower. *Closer!* Chuck vanished in the doorway.

The helicopter descended—until Franklin was
able to grab the big hook and guide it sideways.
At shipyards, cranes lifted these containers off
their chassis and moved them directly onto ships
for transport overseas. An eye was welded at each
corner. It was one of these Franklin wanted.

"Lower!" Everon heard Chuck call out. "Looks
like we're still a couple feet high."

They were very close to the minimum altitude

Everon could risk. A long row of street lights ran along the sides of the bridge. He calculated the distance: *four lanes, each twelve feet wide—forty-eight feet to a side. Two sides: inbound and outbound, a little extra for the center divider—four feet maybe.*

A hundred feet.

In the operating manual tucked behind the seat, the Pelican's blades had been listed at sixty-two. *Blade tips to light poles, less than twenty feet to spare on a side.* Any lower, he'd be down inside them. *One bad gust of wind and—*

More people were being forced over the rails. His left hand made the tiniest dip in the collective.

With a *CLANG!* that vibrated upward, the hook went into the corner eye. Franklin clung to one of the cables.

"He's got it!" Chuck yelled in Everon's ear.

Okay! Everon thought. *Now if we can—* Gently he pulled. The whine of the turbines increased, the blade noise rising with the engine's RPMs. He pulled the collective all the way up. The Pelican strained to rise several feet, then stopped. He waited. The effort was for nothing.

Just the rear of this trailer is too much, he thought. *The Pelican can't lift it!*

"It must be full of something really heavy," Chuck yelled.

"Stop! Stop!" Kone yelled. "You'll kill us all!"

Down below, Franklin shook his head and waved Everon back down.

"Okay," Everon admitted, "maybe this was a bad idea. Tell my brother to cut us loose."

The helicopter descended enough to slack the cables. Franklin pushed the big harness hook from the trailer eye.

The helicopter rose, Franklin's hoist cable retracting with it. It seemed people down there were giving up too. Instead of being crushed to death against the guardrails, they were deliberately jumping off the sides!

At the very moment his feet left the box's roof, he felt hands grip his right leg. A slim woman in her thirties with wavy light hair had somehow gotten to the trailer's top.

Cynthia!

But as the woman struggled to hold on, she looked directly into Franklin's eyes. There was only a vague resemblance. The forehead, the nose. But not the eyes.

Franklin reached to grab her beneath an armpit. But the woman slipped, down onto the screaming crowd, as if diving backward onto fans in a rock concert.

Her soul, Franklin thought, *into the thousands of the screaming damned.*

27

Out Of Control

"What's he doing?" Bonnie Fisk screamed.

She watched the woman fall as air was forced from Bonnie's chest, crushed against a thousand others. She was slowly being pushed toward the bridge's side.

Bonnie wrenched her neck back to look at the man with long dark hair rising toward the helicopter, away from the long orange truck-trailer—as she slid another two feet toward the hole.

"Ahhhheee!" she screamed. Someone's elbow felt like it was going right through her bladder—which reacted, unfortunately, by letting loose, wetting her size-fourteen peach knit slacks. As co-owners of Fiskmart, the sixth largest national chain of retail big box shopping marts, Bonnie and her sister Barbara were worth billions. On the G.W.'s upper deck today, she was no different than anyone else. Mauled and sliding, bumping, moving inexorably *toward that goddamn hole.*

The dark-haired man was leaving them. He was giving up. The helicopter couldn't lift the orange trailer.

Today Bonnie had clung to only one possession. Her keys. And when the dark-haired man beneath the helicopter glanced her way, she put every bit of her considerable strength into throwing them.

They sailed in an arc. Hit him right on the neck.

He stared at her. She pointed.

At the silver container box on the other side of the bridge.

$$\text{\Lightning} \; \dagger$$

Chuck had Franklin halfway up to the Pelican when he saw Franklin wave his right hand and point. He stopped the hoist. Franklin was pointing across the bridge at another 18-wheeler that lay across the outbound lanes. The FedEx and the dumper wedged at its tail against the north bridge railing.

Chuck ducked back to Everon. "He doesn't want to come up! He's pointing to the rear of the silver one!"

"They're too heavy! And that one's got a cab on it too. Reel him in! We have to go back and tell somebody else. Maybe the military can do it."

Chuck hesitated. "Okay."

As Chuck Farndike went for the hoist controls, he felt a tug on his sleeve. Walter van Patter. He leaned his head in close to the billionaire's mouth.

"What color was the first truck?"

"Orange," Chuck answered.

"The orange ones are ocean going," van Patter said. "They're made of steel. The silver ones will be lighter. They're aluminum."

Chuck went forward and told Everon.

Everon doubted they could lift it either.

"Unless it's empty," Chuck said.

Manhattan, Everon knew, was mostly a consumer. *Coming out of the city after a delivery somewhere like the Garment District maybe?* He was sure what Franklin would say. *Look at how many people are down there! Cyn could be one of them—Steve and Melissa, they could* all *be!*

"There's no refrigeration unit either!" Chuck told him. "It's not a meat or fish packer. Might be coming out empty, right?"

"We tried!" Kone complained. "Now let's get out of here!"

"Shut up!" a half dozen voices yelled back.

Everon hovered them directly over the back end of the long silver truck, keeping his blade-to-streetlight distance firmly in mind.

Dangling below the helicopter, Franklin glanced at the sky. Far to the east it looked like the dark cloud had bunched up, upper winds pushing it back into a ball. *It's reversing!*

And then realized suddenly, *I'm descending. They're lowering me back down.*

The soles of his shoes contacted the silver 18-wheeler's top and registered the shaking pressure of the crowd pushing against it.

This time Everon seemed to know how long the cables were below him.

As the helicopter hovered over to the big rig's corner, Franklin quickly pulled the hook with him, slid it into the corner eye farthest from the crowd.

He leaned into one of the lift cables to steady himself. Far east, high in the sky, the cloud vied for his attention.

It's no longer moving away from us! It's coming!

The mob seemed to sense it too. People pushing harder, faster. He could feel it in his feet. *Pressure. The force on each person must be tremendous. No oversold sporting event has ever seen anything like this.* All along the middle of the bridge people were pouring over the sides.

The Pelican began to climb. Everon could feel it in the controls. He was at the top of the lift harness now. Slowly, slowly up the long box came.

"Feels like this one's empty!" he muttered.

A fuel feed light blinked on, glowing above his head. Power on the right turbine gauge dropped out. *"NO! NOT NOW!"*

They were losing power. It felt like the main rotor blades were drooping.

They were going down.

Without thinking, his left hand twisted the throttle, yanked the collective arm upward, until it was angled as high off the floor as he could pull. The other turbine *strained* to keep up, whining, growling, screaming. He eyeballed its temperature gauge as the needle snuck into the red. If they lost the Number One engine here above the bridge like this, rotor blades catching in the bridge piping above these people, it was all over.

No way! Got to get it restarted in the air!

He'd been running the right engine off the rear tank, the left engine off the front. He hit the boost switches. *Too late for that.* Its flame was already out. The rotor continued to lose RPMs.

And then Everon felt the automatic stabilizer system drop out too.

The Pelican rocked in the air, her controls suddenly super-sensitive. Overhead a chip light from the rear crankcase illuminated. He knew what that was. *Pieces of metal getting inside the gearbox. This thing is more of a mess than I realized. We shouldn't even be in the air!*

Down below, Franklin watched with a kind of detached fatalistic awe, the helicopter slowly descending on top of him.

He didn't even have time to move.

† †

Everon glanced at Clarence in the left seat and pointed upward with his chin. "Hit that switch!"

"Which one?" Clarence gulped.

"The one marked right engine boost pump, front tank!"

Clarence flipped it.

"Move that lever," Everon pointed with his eyes to the overhead console. "Twist it! From *left tank*— to *crossfeed*—the right engine."

Clarence moved the lever to the first notch.

"One more!"

The newspaper vendor twisted the black lever all the way over.

"Now this one here," Everon nosed, "the speed selector lever—to SHUTOFF."

He waited a few moments, licked his lips. "Okay, push the start button on Turbine Two."

"Here?" Clarence asked.

"HIT IT!"

Clarence pushed. Nothing.

In back, the transit engineer crossed his fingers in front of himself. The Russians joined him, making the sign of the cross.

Then they all felt it. A vibration.

Everon glanced at the gauge for Turbine Two. The needle jumped. It was restarting. As the rotor's torque increased, the blades felt springier. As the right turbine spun up, he felt a power surge.

They climbed.

Franklin's senses were overwhelmed by the screams of people falling off the sides of the bridge now, screams of people smashed against tractor-trailers, legs and bodies forced against cars, breaking glass, crumpling metal.

He was kneeling on top of the silver trailer, trying to push the big hook out of the box's corner metal eye, when he realized the helicopter's pitch overhead was changing. He looked up. The helicopter's bottom was feet above his head— *But—it doesn't seem to be getting any lower.*

The thick heavy-lift cables tightened. His hand

barely moved in time to keep from getting crushed when the hook yanked itself straight in the box eye.

The trailer's corner, its entire rear end, slowly rose. Higher. Several inches. Without pause, the helicopter immediately moved sideways. The cables grew tighter, pulling the rear of the whole trailer backward. A foot—two feet—dragging its end away from the other truck blocking the road, away from the cars stuck beneath it. And away from the fighting struggling compressed mass of people pressed against it.

The now cheering mob!

As though it were the start of the New York City Marathon—one that might never be run again, like releasing a torrent of water from a breaking dam, thousands burst toward freedom.

And ran with everything they had.

28

A Loss Of Reason

As Franklin was hoisted back up to the Sea Pelican, his eyes studied the bridge's structure, followed the lines of its blue-gray girders, the way they connected. Something he could almost see nagged at him, and faded. *Something—*

Suddenly, in his mind he saw another structure, as it last lay. His brain had snapped a picture at the last possible moment, an image he didn't know he had. If it was still like that when they got— He wouldn't be able to take anything down with him. Did he dare?

Chuck and the Russian Petre swung him through the cargo door.

"We have to go back!" he yelled.

"About time!" said Kone. "We ought to just make it."

"No," said Franklin. "Back to Cynthia's. I know how to get on top!"

"WHAT!" screamed Kone.

"We've already tried twice!" Everon yelled. "Bro," he head pointed, "Look! See that dark stuff out there not making it to the ground? That's virga. It could turn to full-on radioactive rainstorm in an instant. *She's gone!* All that's left to us is to figure out who did it. Vengeance is all we have left and even that's extremely unlikely. *They're gone!* Let them go!"

"They're not! Trust me," Franklin said fiercely. "I know how to get in. Let me try!"

Everon shook his head, lips tight. "This bird's barely in the air."

"You can fly anything."

Everon studied the severe, begging intensity in his younger brother's face. Franklin shouted over the whining engine, "If you don't go back, it's not that I won't forgive you—you'll never forgive yourself!"

Everon's hand left the stick for only a second. To wipe across his eyes.

"You've got to get these people to a hospital first!" Kone yelled.

"If we land, they won't let us take off again," Franklin shouted back.

"What about radiation?" Kone pointed out the Pelican's east windows. "That cloud doesn't look any farther away."

Franklin didn't answer. *It's not. It's closer.*

"Let them have one more try," said van Patter.

"You owe your life to these men, Mr. Kone!" It was Victoria and she pointed a finger at Franklin while looking at the little bureaucrat. "He nearly drowned getting us out! And now you say they can't take every chance, any possibility to find their family?"

Franklin looked at her gratefully. "I didn't know you knew about that."

"The engineer told me," her voice rising to reach Everon. "Put us down somewhere on the Manhattan shore." She pointed at Kone, "Let him walk back!"

Kone yelled. He screamed. He went for the cockpit. At one point Franklin thought he was going to try to wrestle the controls out of Everon's hands.

But with the support of Victoria, of Walter van Patter, the others physically restraining Kone who refused to agree to get out, Everon turned back into Manhattan. They were going back into it. Back toward the cloud.

Bits of ash clung to the Impala's old white body. Edie's left hand gripped Lou's right thigh as she rode next to him in front—while Cheri Enriquez, their new neighbor, tried to comfort her son Johnny in the back.

Kid looks pretty sick, thought Lou Goodman. Another quick look in the rearview mirror. *And his mother isn't looking much better.*

The Goodmans were an old Jewish couple in their seventies, Lou balding, his wife Edith's hair whiter than the Brooklyn snow from the bomb.

They had planned to take the girl and her kid to their son's house in Fort Lee, New Jersey. Lou and Edie's grandkids had moved away to Vegas. Jake and his wife were out there visiting. The apartment was empty.

But a couple miles after they'd left Kings highway, Edith made another whispered suggestion. *"Let's take them to Brooklyn Hospital, Louie. Something's really wrong with that kid."*

Which would have been a good idea. Except the Belt Parkway was out. Not just closed. From what Lou could make out three blocks away, long sections had cracked and slanted out of alignment.

For the next three hours, Lou wound their way through east Brooklyn neighborhoods, and little Johnny got sicker. Cheri too. The young woman was hyperventilating and the kid looked *green.* He couldn't stop crying either.

When they got into Queens, Edie agreed they should give up and try again to get over to Jake's place in Jersey.

But at the George Washington Bridge turnoff, it looked like no one was getting anywhere. And there was still no cellphone signal. When the minivan ahead slowly veered off a northbound exit, Lou followed. *Maybe we can get up across the Tappan Zee Bridge? Drop down into Fort Lee from there?*

Another three hours, traffic channeling them this way, that way. Lou grabbed a look over his shoulder. *Kid isn't breathing too well. Looks sweaty.* Somehow they'd narrowly avoided getting completely stuck, but they weren't making great progress either. They were still in Queens. Lou turned on the radio. The announcer said something about emergency hospital services at Teterboro Airport in New Jersey. *Hmmm* . . .

"Lou! Stop!" Edie screamed. *"Louie! Stop the car!"*

Lou Goodman mashed the brakes as Cheri Enriquez flung open the rear door.

Too late. Little Johnny was already puking his guts out on the back seat. The Goodmans helped Cheri and Johnny outside. The kid was really heaving it up when the thick dark clouds over their heads began to drizzle.

What started as a mist soon thickened. Within a minute all four of them were being pissed on by stinging black rain as the clouds grew even heavier and pushed in toward the city.

29

Cynthia And Steve

The huge ball of fire was still in the way. From the look on Everon's face, the jerky movements of his hands on the controls, the wind had strengthened and was gusting from the east. Out 60th Street, a wall of black mist was moving toward them.

None of it could matter.

"Let me down over there," Franklin pointed. "On that."

Everon took one look. All of two seconds—"No, *no way, Bro!* You can't! It's suicide!"

A falling statue's descent had been arrested by the top of a water tank, on the building separated by the alley behind Cynthia's building. It was some kind of winged creature. *An angel?*

Its feet and the lower tips of its huge flared wings had pierced the tank's round lid. It had come to rest about knee high. One end of a narrow steel

I-beam sat nestled between the arched, protruding top of the broad, curved left wing, and the statue's ugly head.

Not an angel. A stone gargoyle.

The I-beam's other end sat across the alley on the top remaining floor of Cynthia's building. Four stories in the air.

"Even if you find them, how would you get them out?" Everon shouted.

"I'll take some rope, lower them over the side."

Everon was right. He didn't have to do this. He could just stop. *No! He couldn't!*

"I have to know!" he cried. "We have to know!"

"Are you both fucking *crazy?* Is *he?*"

"Hey!" Clarence jumped in at Kone. "Do you realize you're speaking to a—"

"It's okay," Franklin said.

"I don't care if he's the Queen of Sheba." Kone was looking down through the window and let out a piercing, maniacal laugh. "You can't be serious!"

The roly-poly bureaucrat's words hung on the fetid air.

But in his mind, Franklin saw Cynthia, Steve, Melissa, burned, injured, somewhere in the mess below. Victoria, Walter van Patter, the others were watching him.

"Am I crazy?" he said. "Maybe right now a little."

But Kone's doubt seemed to buck Everon up. Everon shook his head, lips pinched. "I'll get you as close as I can." He turned northward, then hovered them over the middle of a twenty-yard gap.

Franklin slung a coil of rope over one shoulder.

"Isn't that rain?" Kone pointed through the east windows. "Is that radioactive? That can't be more than a mile or two away!"

"Ready on the hoist," Chuck said, a determined pressure visible around the big man's mouth.

Franklin hooked his harness to the cable with a carabiner then swung himself through the Pelican's wide doorway. This time he was ready for the freezing rotor blast. Chuck pressed the down button. Franklin began to drop.

His toes touched down on a wobbly beam more than three stories in the air. Franklin centered his mass, feet sideways, single file. The beam's top was only inches wide. It hadn't come to rest flat but angled slightly upward toward Cynthia's building. A foul-smelling wind took his hair behind him, pushed at his chest, his shoulders. He stood wavering, knees bent, hands out trying to find his balance.

As Chuck slowly let out more line, Franklin took a deep breath and released his harness from the hoist cable.

He took another breath and slid his right foot forward. Left foot step. A long way down to the jagged pile of junk at the bottom. Slide-step. *What am I doing? Maybe Kone's right. I must be out of my mind.*

His only safety net was to fall on his chest or arms and try to hang on. This was the craziest thing he had ever done.

The girder wobbled. *Or is it the statue? Is it slipping?*

He waited. The rope coiled over his shoulder made balance difficult.

Step. Slide-step.

It would be no worse than the splat falling from Ash Cave.

Heights had once bothered him. Years ago he had found a way to fool part of his mind into thinking he was only a few feet in the air.

Step. Slide-step.

He caught the beam's rhythm and moved faster. As long as he remained in some way connected to the ground he was okay.

He. Was. Across!

As he stepped off the beam's edge onto open floor, the beam slid backwards, statue disappearing into the water tank. He watched his end of the long beam fall end-over-end into the alley below.

The fireball flared and he felt the heat against his cheek. On his other side, wind from the rotor blades whipped up a storm of swirling garbage. The floor shook, vibrating—each step like walking on poorly supported plywood.

Has to be concrete, though, doesn't it? he thought, waving Everon away.

The helicopter moved up the block, the blades still loud but his footing didn't vibrate so much.

Dark smoke drifted across what was left of Cynthia's apartment. Twisted pieces of metal, piles of block from other buildings. *Definitely the right place though. Strange, the file cabinet wasn't touched.* It sat by itself against a chunk of one remaining exposed brick wall.

There seemed to be no other sign of Cynthia or Steve or Melissa. Areas of jaggedly broken brick wall still separated the apartment from its neighbors— he wondered if he really was standing in the right one. The thick smoke stung his eyes, burned his nostrils. *Isn't their bedroom across from the room this cabinet was in? Could the cabinet have moved?*

For a moment a breeze blew the smoke away, and the corner of the pink blanket he'd noticed from the chopper protruding from the third file cabinet drawer, waved in the wind. And then, two apartments over, his eye caught on a roll of burned cloth, seven or eight feet long, three feet in diameter.

He felt himself being pulled toward it.

Some type of garbage, an old rolled-up rug.

But it was too familiar. He knew that pattern. Too well.

The blackened outside let only a little of the bright colors show through—in small places— yellow and orange, green and red and blue. A comforter. A Mexican blanket. The edge of a woven design. A giant round Aztec calendar stone that he knew filled the entire center.

He knelt down. There was a large dark stain across its middle he'd never seen before. A scratching, sucking sound as he carefully peeled back the crisp outer layer.

And his sister's eyes opened to him.

"Cynthia!"

30

Cynthia

"Franklin," Cynthia coughed. "I thought I was—I didn't think anyone would—" Tears streamed from the corners of her eyes. Face-to-face inside the cocoon with Franklin's sister was her husband.

Franklin looked at Steve. Felt his cheek. It was cold. Ice-water cold. He wasn't breathing. He was gone.

Cynthia laughed bitterly, began to cry, "He went an hour ago," she coughed, struggled to pull a breath. "My arms . . . I . . . couldn't move."

At least I can still save Cynthia, Franklin thought. They were wrapped so tightly, Cynthia's arms pinned to her sides. "Here, let me get you out of—" he began, unwrapping the blanket—

"Ahhhh!" Cynthia cried, "Don—don't!"

But Franklin had already peeled it open far enough to see.

A piece of metal he hadn't noticed, barely protruding from the outsides of the charred blanket, had pierced them both. The only difference being it had gone through Steve slightly more in the center of his chest. Cynthia's wound was more to the right side.

"I've had better nights-out in New York," Cynthia rasped out with a weak smile. Her attempts to ignore the obvious pain were betrayed by her ragged gasping for air. Her lips were turning blue.

Franklin looked around wildly, up to the helicopter. The black rain was closing fast. By the sound of her breathing, Cynthia's right lung was punctured. *How do I get her out of here? How can I get her over the building's side, down to the street? Without killing her?*

Everon must be able to see.

He waved frantically, trying to will Everon in closer. But the ball of flame expanded, driving the helicopter back. He could just imagine how Kone was responding.

It looked like Everon was going to try another tack, come around back, inside the block.

Cynthia's eyes shot to her left. "The cab—" The word died on her lips. Her eyes rolled back in her head. A long gurgling breath poured from her mouth.

"No . . . Cynthia!"

Franklin grasped his sister's head. But he knew that sound too well. He'd heard it from the throats of too many dying Rangers. A death rattle. His sister was gone.

He held his sister's shoulders in his lap, a hand under Cynthia's head. He threw up on the dusty floor. He'd found them too late. *If only I'd gotten here thirty minutes sooner.* An hour the subway had cost him. *Another hour at the damn bridge. Would I have been able to save both of them? Did I actually kill Cynthia by unwrapping the blanket, removing the pressure that held her together?*

He let out a long, deep exhale. Tears flowed from his eyes, down his face, onto his chin, his mouth gasping for air.

His sister and brother-in-law's naked bodies still clutched each other, holding each other tightly. Cynthia's blonde, conservative banker's hair; the short dark hair matted about Steve's head—he brushed a couple of flies angrily away from Cynthia's face. But for the blood at the corner of Cynthia's mouth, in the midst of smoke and fire and the ultimate violence, they were only sleeping.

She had always quoted one verse to him, a Proverb: *Above all your possessions, value understanding.* Cynthia's humor had been a door to that understanding. And what she'd always said to understand was that everything—*every effect*—had a cause. That every cause was a value. And *values*, were completely personal. Cynthia had been one of Franklin's highest values—besides God—a major cause, a reason for living. And now that link to his family, to their mother and to Everon even, was gone.

His arms twisted. Like being forced to chew a jalapeño pepper whole while someone used a hammer to break both his arms and legs, unbearable agony coursed through his entire body. Some distant part of him knew the pain in his every cell was purely mental. He didn't want to think. *About anything anymore.* His altruistic gamble may have saved a bunch of strangers, but it had cost him his sister's life. There was nothing he could do. No magic formula. No prayer. No take-backs. This was it. Cynthia was gone.

I have to get them out of here.

He would lower them to the ground, then himself. Chuck could pick them up there. He looked over the building's edge. But the street was flooding.

From the helicopter, Everon watched the low dark tide rushing down the avenue. Flooding into side streets. Reaching Cynthia's building.

"Aren't there big water supply tunnels under the city?" Chuck asked.

"The water's gravity-fed," Walter van Patter answered. "It comes down from the Catskill Mountains. If the tunnels have cracked open, there's no stopping it."

"We'll have to leave him!" Kone screamed hysterically.

WHOOM! The sound of fire imploding echoed, rocking the floor beneath Franklin's feet. Out in the street, the huge gas ball of fire shrank back again . . . to nothing. The flame was out!

He squatted there, looking around, shocked by the sudden loss of noise and heat. He blew some air from his nostrils, wiped his eyes.

He looked up at the helicopter, then back to the bodies. He could just imagine what Everon was going to say—*to think.*

Everon must see him. There was nothing either of them could do now. He quickly cut a piece of rope, tugged the burned edge of the Aztec comforter back into place and began winding the rope around and around them, binding the entire thing like a cocoon.

The black wall, nuclear rain out 60th, was nearly on them. Everon was already bringing the helicopter over.

Franklin hooked the bundle onto the cable and gave Chuck the signal. The cocoon lifted skyward. Franklin looked around to see if he might have missed anything. There was no sign of Melissa. No bassinet, nothing.

☥ ✝

Above his head, Franklin watched Chuck swing the wrapped bodies through the helicopter door. The storm was bearing down on them. Wind blasting in sudden gusts.

As he waited for Chuck to send the cable back down for him, he noticed a shaking brown mass the shape of a small football by the base of the file cabinet. *What's that?* he wondered.

It turned its head.

Some sort of bird, he realized. The exotic brown and white pattern across its feathers fluttered in the strengthening wind. Huge yellow eyes peered up at him as it shivered against the cabinet. *An owl?*

He reached out to touch it. *Doesn't seem afraid or aggressive.* He scooped a hand underneath, gently lifting it, sliding his wrist against the cabinet.

And then he heard something—a crying sound.

"The cabinet—"

Pivoting his ears back and forth—*from inside?*

His eyes locked on the flapping pink material caught in the second drawer. Holding the bird in one hand, he tried to pull it open. To *force* it open. He tried them all. None of them would budge. The oval-shaped lock was sticking out. *Unlocked position.* He lowered his head—*loudest from the second drawer!*

She's in here! She's alive!

The side of the file cabinet was warm. He could feel the heat right through the glove on his hand. *The fireball.*

Using the hook knife from his harness, he pried into the crack along the drawer's side—hoping at least to bend the drawer outward far enough to confirm his suspicions. The black edge widened to an eighth of an inch.

Snap! The curved blade broke halfway back.

He looked desperately for some way to get the drawer open. *Dammit! A whole tool kit in the helicopter, a screwdriver, a pry bar—*

Before he realized what was happening, the building's entire floor suddenly shifted—he felt his thigh and calf muscles react, even before his conscious mind. "Ahhh!" He felt the whole building wobble as if the foundation of life were cracking beneath his feet.

His first thought was to grab for the cabinet handles, but the floor steadied at a slight angle, maybe five degrees. The foundation rumbled deep somewhere below. *Damn, this thing could go any time! Why am I swearing? Too much time spent around Everon. Starting to affect me.*

He waved frantically for Everon to fly the cable over the cabinet. The dark misty rain looked less than two or three blocks away.

As Chuck lowered the cable, Franklin quickly unbuttoned the middle of his white shirt and stuffed one of the few living creatures he'd seen today, the owl, inside. He used what was left of the hook knife to cut a piece of rope. He looped the rope through the cabinet's four drawer handles and tied the ends together.

The wind blasted. The cable hook whacked him on the shoulder.

He snagged it onto the rope. Pulled on the handles to test their strength. They looked like they would hold. He stretched the connecting loop of his own harness to the cable hook. The floor shook violently and with a rumble, as if in slow motion—all he could do to throw both hands around the cable, himself onto the cabinet—the floor fell away.

And the building collapsed below.

His arms felt like they were being pulled from

their sockets. His body stretched over the top of the cabinet as the lift cable dug through his gloves, into the palms of his hands. He felt a sharp pain beneath his shirt. The owl had latched its talons into his stomach. He moved his knees against the cabinet to keep pressure off the bird. The pain in his midsection eased off.

Overhead blades whipping at his dark hair, the hoist reeled Franklin skyward.

While the cabinet's handles might have been strong enough to support the cabinet, they now had to carry his weight as well. He couldn't get enough grip on the hard stainless cable to pull himself away. The angle, the bird, all combined to make it impossible. But he was rising.

Fifteen feet from the opening in the side of the helicopter, unable to see what was happening below his dangling feet, he felt something sag. With a loud *BANG!* the bottom handle ripped loose. It felt like the cabinet was going to keep going. But the next lowest drawer handle held—and immediately began to bend.

"Oww!" Franklin yelled as the bird dug into his flesh, this time into his ribs. The little owl was getting rambunctious in there, rummaging around under his shirt. He tried to suck in his stomach but it was all he could do to just hang on . . .

Out the open helicopter side door, Chuck could see what was happening. But the hoist had one speed—slow. Chuck mentally willed it to go faster.

He shouted to Everon, "You'd better find a safe

place to get this thing on the ground before that cabinet drops off there. Looks like he's got it connected by its handles. And they're tearing out!"

$$\dot{\underline{\wedge}} \; \dot{\dagger}$$

The wind blew.

Out Everon's front window, the deadly black rain was closing. Almost near enough to touch. The weight of the swinging cabinet made the helicopter dance despite radical corrections to the controls in Everon's hands.

"There's just no good place, Chuck, the way it's swinging. The wind's picking up from the east causing turbulence around these buildings. That black rain's closing in. We can't go back to the fountain—there's no other place the blades can fit around here. Isn't he almost in?"

As the top of the cabinet cleared the helicopter's floor, Clarence reached out to swing it in—and slipped. Like slow motion, he was falling out the door—twenty degrees past vertical when the transit engineer snagged a grip on his shirt, and yanked him back inside.

Petre the Russian, on the wide door's other side, reached for Franklin's harness. Franklin tried to swing a foot around to step inside.

Plunk!

One side of the second lowest handle—on the drawer he thought she might be inside—chose that moment to rip away.

The rope slipped around it. With a scraping jar, the big metal box slid a foot-and-a-half down against the lower doorframe. Now the top two handles carried the load.

If I could just get my weight off it! He could barely hold onto the rope with one hand. The Russian, Clarence, Chuck and the engineer tried to grab the box's smooth sides to haul him in.

He could feel the rope slipping beneath his chest, the next handle bending. Every time he pulled himself off the cabinet the owl seemed to dig into his stomach deeper. He ignored the talons and hung off the top of the cable hook using only his biceps.

The hoist wound more cable. It was high enough!

Chuck, Clarence, the engineer and the Russian moved fast. The third handle snapped, just as they pulled the box through the door. *Bang!*—the cabinet fell to the open edge of the helicopter's metal floor, teetering, twisting on the edge as four pairs of hands struggled to wrestle the tall metal box all the way inside.

"He's in!" Chuck yelled to Everon, amongst cheering passengers—all but Kone who demanded, "What in hell did you bring that up for?"

Everon stabilized the chopper and climbed gently away from the black mist. They were getting short on fuel. He tapped the oil gauge. It didn't look like the leak was getting any better either.

Victoria was closest. She leaned her head on the warm cabinet. *"I hear crying!"*

"What?" Kone yelled.

"Crying! Inside! Here!" she said, pointing at the second drawer from the bottom.

"The second drawer!" Clarence said, "She's right!"

"Da!" echoed the Russian woman Kat, her head next to Victoria's.

Franklin was already jumping for tools from the helicopter's rear wall. Flipping open the toolbox lid, ignoring a hammer, screwdrivers and wrenches, near the bottom he found a two-foot pry bar.

He dropped an ear against the cabinet's side. To his relief, despite the helicopter blades and engines, he could still hear that crying sound. He put the bar's edge into the narrow gap along the right side and pushed. The metal side bent outward, creating a small triangular gap. He pulled on the drawer. It still wouldn't slide open.

He put one eye to the opening. *Can't see!* he thought furiously.

He wedged the bar into the slit along the drawer's top. Its horizontal divider bent as much as the drawer itself, then with a sudden *clanggg!*— popped outward.

Chuck, Walter van Patter, Victoria, Clarence, the Russians, the transit engineer, even Kone, jockeyed to see as Franklin struggled to scrape out the damaged drawer, screeching metal-against-metal audible above the helicopter's noise.

Between the fourth and fifth buttons on Franklin's white button-down shirt, a fluffy brown and white speckled head poked its way out to join the curious.

And there she was, wrapped in a pink blanket,

nestled between a few hanging file folders, face-to-face with the exotically colored bird, crying with all the gusto she could manage—Franklin and Everon's baby niece, Melissa.

31

Dead Man Walking

He wasn't sure if the storm outside had calmed some. His cabin was steadier. If anything his stomach felt worse.

Ahmad Hashim rolled his face over the side of his bunk and vomited more of the viscous green and red fluid into a rusty metal bucket. He sucked down ragged gasps of air, trying to relax. *More red than green this time. Blood,* he knew. The skin across his stomach, chest and shoulders was a boiling rash. He put a hand to his burning forehead.

No! He would *not* do it again. *So many dead. So many brothers and sisters. Why was it only the Jews Allah told the killing of one innocent man was as the killing of the entire world? Why have I done this thing? No amount of money is worth this guilt, this pain.* He had made a terrible choice and Allah had made this sickness his price.

Ahmad closed his eyes and lay his dark curly

hair and blistering neck back on the bunk. *My own guilt it was that allowed such a foolish error.*

A criticality accident, it was called. It seemed to be getting more difficult to—his memory seemed to be going—*too much plutonium in too small a space . . . trying to modify the device—the halves of the bomb's core in too close proximity with one another . . . radiation filling the lab. Shooting through the walls . . .* anyone within twenty feet in all directions would be as he was now.

Hashim had been the only one. Except for the bird, of course.

The lab shared a wall with the Evil One's own cabin. *Too bad the Evil One was not in there too,* Hashim thought viciously. Only the bird, and now Hashim's friend Taliq had taken it. *Does the infidel even know his bird is gone?* Hashim certainly wasn't going to tell him.

His stomach rumbled, ready to release again. *Na'am—yes! Eighty, ninety miles. Certainly we are less than a hundred off the East Coast. Allah will guide me.* Ahmad would find someone and warn them about what was coming. He had to try. He must remove himself from this ship. If he did not receive outside medical attention he would not last another day.

He slid his feet from the bunk and forced himself unsteadily erect. Struggled into a jacket. Slid the two candy bars, a small bottle of water into his right jacket pocket. His left held the control cards.

As he staggered to the cabin door, Ahmad slipped on the vile green slop. The doorknob caught the side of his head painfully but his hands grasped it and kept him on his feet.

At the stairs he crawled his way up each stair, pulling himself up the railing for support . . .

Up to the starboard side of the main deck— where the four white boats hung from their davits above the water. He looked over the side.

Norse Wind was making more than fifteen knots against a five-knot wind. *Even with help, dangerous to launch at this speed.* He was alone and he had no choice.

Two days earlier, Ahmad had watched the transmitter men leave. The outdated lifeboat had no upper shell. Only a cloth tarp cover that looked old enough to have come off the *Titanic*. When Ahmad doubted its condition, the man enthusiastically explained, *"Nothing to worry about, my friend. If need be, all is automatic. One sets the timer—we push this button here, then this one . . ."*

Slow eight-foot swells rose along *Norse Wind's* side. *They will be to my advantage,* Ahmad thought dully, a hacking snort erupting from his nose. *If I live through launch.*

He set the controls for self-launch then crawled up inside. He had to get off without anyone else seeing. The Evil One, no doubt, would kill him for desertion. And sabotage.

As the mechanism unwound, with what strength he had left, he struggled to remove the rear of the white tarp from its hooks before the boat hit the water.

The boat slapped down and Ahmad jolted forward, but the still-connected tarp caught his knees and saved him from launching into the air.

He grabbed the starboard rail and removed the aft winch cable. Pulled himself across the tarp to reach the bow hook before the next trough could yank him airborne, but the cable released itself. And he watched as the huge ship rolled away—then loomed dangerously back, inches from crushing his tiny vessel.

The gap widened. He left the front of the tarp attached. *Better to keep water out,* he thought. He hurried the key, surprised to hear the motor come to life on its first try. He pushed the tiller to steer away west.

WHOOOSH, a sound blasted from the ship's hull. He looked up to see a long dark object flying from the narrow side door in the ship's bow, land in the water and disappear.

The second fish launched! *"Oh, Allah, no!"*

32

The Dolls

Sal Torentino kept an eye on his wife in the craziness through the Chevy's windshield.

Both their cellphones were still NO SIGNAL at the Utica, New York exit. There was power here, and in the long lines at the three scarce pay phones that seemed to be working, Margarete was still near the back. She had insisted they stop and try to call her mother.

Like many of their neighbors, Sal's family of four had evacuated Westchester north of the city with the blare of the first siren. Sal was Italian, but he had screamed at his wife and kids for the first time in, well—ever. Trying to hurry them into the car as the Emergency Alert Station played on the car radio. Screeching out of the driveway, down the street, out of their neighborhood to the highway and going—nowhere fast.

What should have taken two hours had taken an exhausting twelve.

People were being turned away at the door of the Denny's. They were obviously out of food. So were the Torentinos. The sodas and beer, the sandwiches Margarete made for them on the road were long gone. Sal had found some rock-hard candy bars in a vending machine.

Six hours ago.

When he couldn't function anymore, Margarete had driven. If you could call it that. Jammed between a thousand other cars. Five and ten miles an hour.

A tremendous sense of relief poured into Sal Torentino as the sun came out from under an overcast blanket of gray-white. Thankfully the kids were so tired they were silent, curled up across the back seat, the tops of their heads touching. He smiled. *We're all so beat,* he thought. He'd checked every half hour or so to make sure they weren't dead or something back there. In a minute the sun was gone. *Another winter storm coming in.*

Across the freeway, people were driving the wrong way—*against no traffic*—moving a lot faster than Sal had been.

Somebody up ahead laid on their horn.

"*Whoa!* Looks like they smashed into each other halfway up the ramp," he said softly.

Then the sound hit him, a series of screams two drivers were throwing at each other. "Clear the goddamned road you two motherfuckingsonsabitches!" another voice yelled.

The accident drivers looked up, turned their heads back to each other.

The door of a black Mercedes immediately behind them flew open. The driver ran toward the two crashers. In seconds, name-calling accelerated into a three-way fistfight. The smaller of the original two dove sideways. The Mercedes driver and the bigger man wrestled each other to the ground. The smaller guy watched while the other two rolled down the snowy slope along the ramp.

"Look, Daddy!" Sal's kids screamed with excitement.

Dammit! Now the kids are awake!

Sal's left elbow flinched. A horse walked almost touching the left side of the car, right along the windows. What looked to Sal—the harness blinkers, the odd saddle, he was no expert—like a shiny-red thoroughbred racehorse.

The black tail swished into view. When the beast was farther along Sal could see the rider's legs. The big man was no jockey, a broad back in an expensive black leather jacket, urging his animal past the brawlers, out onto the freeway.

"Where we going, Daddy?" Sal Torentino's five-year old boy asked from the back seat.

"Shhhhh," Sal answered. "Go back to sleep."

But they didn't want to go back to sleep. "Where are we going, Daddy?" Sal's six-year-old daughter cooed.

Sal didn't answer right away. He didn't know what to answer. And he didn't want to scare them.

He checked the phones. Margarete was almost to the front.

"Where we going? Where we going?" his son joined in.

They're not going to stop, are they? Sal realized, pushing his back teeth against each other. *Some kind of answer. Quiet them down maybe.* "We're going for a drive." The words were out of his mouth before he knew what he'd done.

"We're going for a drive, we're going for a drive . . . "

For the next ten minutes the kids chanted like idiot monks.

"Going for a drive, going for a drive!"

Sal finally exploded. "Shut up back there!" He rarely lost his temper. Almost never with the kids. But they shut up.

"Feathee!" Sal's daughter held up a long feather painted with streaks of dark tan.

"Where—!"

She was cramming her dolls into that yellow tool box he'd rescued from the restaurant.

"Gimme!" said Sal's son.

"Mine!" his daughter whisked the feather an inch out of his son's reach. She put it back in with her dolls. The lid slammed.

The toolbox took up the whole of the floor on the side behind Sal's seat. His daughter's legs were short enough that resting her feet on its lid probably made sitting more comfortable for her. He'd forgotten all about it. *The feather must have been inside.*

He recalled the small boat pulling up to tie at the restaurant's dock. The Middle Eastern man opening the toolbox, releasing that bird—an owl, it looked like—into the air beneath the Brooklyn Bridge. The man leaving the box after he ate lunch.

Margarete came back looking more frazzled than ever. "I couldn't get through to Momma in Rochester, Saly!" She closed her door— "I couldn't reach Momma! Oh I'm so worried about her." She frowned at the kids. "Anything happen? Kids okay?"

"Not much," Sal swallowed. "They're fine. I'm sure she's okay. We'll try again in a little while."

"She's probably worried sick." She turned. "Want to go see Momma Conti, kids?"

They perked right up. "Momma Conti! Momma Conti!"

Rita looked at him, a line down her pretty forehead. "I'm sure she'll be glad to have us—so happy to see the kids, Saly—"

Sal sighed. "Okay. Daniella's it is."

But the freeway entrance was blocked.

Sal carefully snuck his tires up over the rounded curb of the left berm, easing the Chevy partway up the angled concrete. The space on the left was just enough to squeeze their right fender around one fighter as he bumped the other into the bushes.

"Saly!"

"I only nudged him—"

Sal's big shoulders sagged. He let out a big breath as the Torentinos slid into traffic. Again.

33

Return To Jersey

Clarence, the Russian and the transit engineer pulled the heavy hook and most of its cable back into the Pelican, tying them with a piece of climbing rope to one of the bench seat supports along the side. They closed the cargo door as far as the lift harness would allow and the freezing wind dropped to a light roar.

Cradled in Franklin's arms, Melissa wiggled, a secret smile on her face. Fine blonde hair like Cynthia's. She acted as though she were safe, the most comfortable baby in the world. How long had she been wearing that same night outfit? *More than sixteen hours,* he guessed. He could smell something going on in there. Not much he could do about *that* right now. He worried why she hadn't complained about not being fed for what must have been, *what? More than twelve hours?*

Since he'd taken her from the cabinet, the only

time she cried was when he tried to have someone else hold her. He would only need a moment to reach inside his shirt and pull out the bird. But Melissa would go wild. He felt another brief scamper, claws against his skin. The bird had ducked back inside and it wouldn't come out either. *Wish I could get it out of my shirt.*

As they cleared the Hudson River cliffs re-entering New Jersey, Everon breathed a little easier. *At least I won't have to make a water landing.* He could set them down in any open field, if he had to, even a golf course, a parking lot.

Noise was increasing, the *left* turbine's tachometer needle this time pegging into the red. He knew what *that* meant—*governor's failing to the high side*—*a runaway engine. If there isn't smoke trailing us yet, there will be soon.*

He didn't want to do it— He grabbed the left turbine lever and slid it back to MANUAL. There was no effect. He took a deep breath. *No choice at all now.* He couldn't just wait for the right engine to self-destruct. Still, he hesitated, calculating quickly—*thirteen passengers. Burned off a lot of fuel. Nowhere near overload. Still have one engine.*

He reached over, slid the left turbine control to OFF and cut its boost pumps. Immediately the Pelican began to sink as the right turbine spun down. He compensated by increasing pressure on the collective, pushing the right turbine harder, forcing the helicopter to hold altitude.

In the distance he spotted the eight-story red-brick Med Center, north of the airport. He'd seen their heliport marked on a map. *Probably less than three miles,* he guessed. *Still one good engine.*

He adjusted the radio frequency. "Helicopter Pelican Two-Two-Bravo-India, emergency approach for Hackensack Med Center Roof Top Heliport."

He waited. There was no answer. "Med Center Heliport, do you read?"

As the red-brick building moved closer he could make out another chopper still sitting on the roof! Its blades weren't even turning!

A voice came back to him. "Uh— Bravo-India we read, we're closing except to Teterboro high-risk patient transfers. Delay several minutes."

He couldn't delay even one minute. Everon veered for the airport.

Much of the space around the runways was occupied by tents. *Must be an awful lot of casualties coming in.* Then he noticed he'd been unconsciously raising his left arm and the Pelican's collective with it. *"Losing power?"* he blurted. He glanced at the altimeter. "A thousand feet," he muttered to no one in particular. They shouldn't have been but they *were* dropping. He glanced at the engine instruments. *Shit!* The right turbine's fuel filter light was on again. *We're going down!*

He scanned the area quickly. *All I need is a little—*

There was an oblong-shaped corner of the airport still open, several helicopters there already. *Can I glide it that far?* And then he heard that harsh, asshole voice again—

"Where are you planning to land? I hope you're taking us directly to the hospital," Kone yelled.

"We're losing altitude goddammit!" Everon snarled through his teeth. "This thing'd fly a whole lot better with less weight. Care to step outside, Mr. Kone?"

"Please be quiet," Franklin whispered forcefully to the little bureaucrat. "You're not helping."

Perspiration dripped from Everon's forehead. "Hold on!" he yelled and lowered the collective to the floor.

As if the bottom dropped out, the Pelican fell. *Fast.*

No one said a word.

34

Falling Down

Houses rose toward them—*a baseball diamond. Could I make that? Too far. That parking lot? Power lines.* Everon fought himself not to white-knuckle the machine, to continue *feeling* the controls.

"It's going to be close," he muttered.

Franklin kept one eye on Melissa, the other on his brother's face. He couldn't recall ever having seen Everon like this, this—pure focused rage it looked like—none of his typical sarcastic humor. Franklin's fingers slid off the triangle base of the small gold cross beneath his shirt, then brushed the soft feathers of the owl's head.

And then he saw it clearly. It had been a personally dangerous, altruistic and foolhardy thing they'd done to release all those people on the bridge. He and Everon had put their own lives at risk out of grief and desperation. *Thinking we'd failed Cynthia and Steve. How could I have let these strangers become more important than my own sister?*

Now that they were certain Cynthia was dead, Franklin felt a kind of pure, blind hatred like nothing he'd ever felt before. But nobody knew who to hate. Only a desperate need to somehow strike back, do something drastic.

In the co-pilot seat to Everon's left, Clarence's hands clenched around the base of his seat cushion. He felt his stomach rise, the ground coming toward them at an alarming rate, trees, buildings—*Fuck! I knew I should have worn the green shirt yesterday! Life is always better, safer in the green shirt!* But it was so hard to sell newspapers when he was smelly.

Down ahead of Everon, a power line appeared across their path. But they were committed. A messy crash—death for everyone if he snagged it. He pushed the yoke forward.

They fell faster.

The transit engineer looked at his digital wristwatch. Strange. He hadn't noticed. The numbers hadn't changed. *Eight-zero-zero. Does it mean something? Can't be good. Stomach feels like it's in my throat.* Certain numbers had always been lucky for him. Never double zero.

Are we going to make it past this power line? Everon asked silently. With no engine, they were dropping on a steep angle, free-falling, only a small amount of resistance from the main rotor, in full auto-rotate. *No time to bring the tail around.* He jerked hard back on the yoke. Shoulders hunched, Everon pulled his head into his neck waiting for the tail to strike.

Despite cold air whistling through the cracks, small bubbles of perspiration formed on Tyner Kone's upper lip. As the Pelican fell, he rushed to make certain he was balanced. With his right hand, nervously he tapped his left shoulder, then more softly with his left hand tapped his right. *Too hard on the left,* he thought. *Must have balance!*

There was no deadly tilt, no sudden jerk. Ground flying at them, Everon's left hand yanked on the collective arm almost ripping it from the floor.

The Russian woman Kat felt like suddenly she weighed a thousand pounds. Despite the security of Petre's arm around her shoulder, she had known this was how it would end for them since yesterday. That flock of pitch-black crows in Queens landing on a street pole, beaks cawing loudly—*right at her! The most evil sign!* A warning she hadn't under-stood—*until now! The bomb! The subway! To die finally smashed into the ground!*

They slammed in hard. Then *bounced!* Off the Pelican's balloon tires—six, eight, ten feet in the air. Then fell, hit again, not so hard this time, and *settled*—to near stillness.

Everon's breath shot from his lips. *FFFFffff . . .* like air going from the tires. He looked around.

"Alright back there?"

"We're okay!" Franklin yelled.

"Well I'm not—"

But for the semiconscious Walter van Patter, the again bitching Tyner Kone, they all clapped and cheered.

They were on the airport runway. A hundred feet from the nearest tent.

35

The Press

Of the people running toward the helicopter, Franklin spotted several hauling video cameras. *Photographers and reporters.* The rest, wearing pale hospital greens, carried stretchers, pushed wheelchairs. They helped Walter van Patter, now conscious again, into one; Victoria Hill into another.

"Which one of you's a doctor?" Kone whined indignantly. "I feel like I'm ready to fall over, after everything *I've* been through!"

The wind was calm in New Jersey, Franklin noticed. Just as it had been at the fountain minutes before it changed directions. The black cigar-shaped cloud jutted out. *Has it reached the river? How much time does it leave us to get out?*

Everon pulled one of the medic's collapsible stretcher dollies next to the cargo door. Franklin got to his feet with Melissa. His jacket halfway open, the owl poked its head out between his white shirt's middle two buttons again. A photographer snapped a picture. The flash scared the bird back inside.

"You have an *owl* in there!" a reporter pointed.

"I found him on top of an apartment building," Franklin muttered.

"We should call him Harry!" Victoria spoke up. "In honor of our narrow escape." She pointed to Melissa. "Harry helped find this little girl!"

Flashes flashed. Video cameras recorded. Vandersommen, that same jerk airport security guard who nearly stopped them going into the city, emerged from the crowd. Before he could say anything, Everon said, "Emergency landing. Lost both engines. No choice."

"You had no authorization in the first place." Vandersommen wrote something in a small notebook, while looking at the Pelican's tail number.

An Army major ran over followed by two of his men. "We're commandeering this helicopter!"

"Go ahead!" Everon barked. He jumped down from the big cargo door. With Chuck's help, they began to wrestle the Aztec cocoon out onto the dolly.

Franklin heard someone shout, "Victoria!" One of the reporters apparently knew her. He pushed a microphone to her face. Clarence nudged behind Victoria's chair, freeing the woman in green scrubs.

"We better hustle," Everon said as he and Chuck passed alongside with the Aztec cocoon. "Look!" he head-pointed. The dark cloud looked to be completely across the Hudson. "By the time that gets here we better be long gone! Meet you at the jet, Bro!"

Before anyone could thank them, Everon and Chuck pushed ahead.

"You were rescued by these men, Ms. Hill?"

"They pulled us out of a collapsed subway. They're amazing."

"And these EMS personnel are from where?" another reporter asked.

"They're brothers," Clarence cut in. "The pilot's from Vegas." He pointed at Franklin. "He's a Congregational minister."

"A *what?*" Victoria looked at Franklin, as surprised as the reporter.

"The big guy told me," Clarence nodded at Chuck, pointed back at Franklin. "The dark-haired one is *Reverend* Franklin Reveal. The blond surfer guy's the pilot, Everon Student. They saved us— and about three hundred thousand other people."

"How's *that?*" the reporter asked. "Three hundred *thousand—?*"

Franklin walked faster.

"Be ready to expect a *lot* more survivors in about an hour!" the transit engineer put in. "They set thousands free when they opened a path on top of the G.W."

Communications must be out, Franklin realized. *Nobody even knows what's happening.*

He passed soldiers adding to a row of tall green and white toilets. One woman lined up said to another behind her, "I just hate these porta-things, don't you?"

Through the nearest tent's entrance, Franklin saw people crammed on ankle-high cots. Doctors and nurses clearly past overload, bandaging foreheads, arms, legs. Selecting who would live, and who could not be helped, who would die. Franklin thought of the mob coming from the bridge.

People were crying, screaming, searching for the ones they'd lost. As if someone had torn away the reality in which they'd lived. The world was upside down, where nothing made any sense at all.

"Yea, *brother!*" shouted a homeless vagrant in tattered clothes and cutoff gloves, voice rising like an old-time revivalist. "The end of days is come!"

Mania was taking over.

An elderly bleached-blonde stepped in Franklin's way. A camel-shaped brown stain ran across the bottom of her long torn skirt. Her right hand parallel with the ground just above her head, she asked, "White-hair, about this tall—have you seen my husband? They said they would bring him on the next helicopter . . . " her thick Jewish-Brooklyn accent trailed off.

"No, I'm sorry," Franklin answered.

She wandered away screaming violently, "WHO HAS *DONE* THIS!"

No one told her to be quiet. It was the same question they were all asking. There was no victim list you could check to see if someone you cared about was on it. He doubted there ever could be such a list. There were so many like her. People who seemed not to know where they were or what they were doing. Only that something important had been taken from their lives. *"Oh, please God . . ."* voices trailed off nearby. A total loss of reason.

"What was it like over there?" a female reporter asked, pushing a microphone into Franklin's face.

He stepped around her.

Franklin had no desire to talk about the city. He didn't want to hate Vandersommen or this reporter or anybody. The only person he hated was someone he couldn't see or touch or find. Someone who had set off a bomb that had caused fire and agony and so much pain.

36

Who's Responsible?

The mob of G.W. Bridge survivors was halfway to Teterboro when drops of black goo began to fall from the sky. Fifty-one people squeezed in together atop a narrow raised concrete oval that housed the pumps of a Quick-N-Go GAS U-POURIUM.

On the platform's front side, barely protected by the station's overhang, the woman who'd hit Franklin with her keys struggled to keep her weight off her bloody right leg without being pushed off the pump platform into the growing black muck. Bonnie Fisk's torn pants did not protect her from the goo's backsplash, each cold ricocheted drop a little bit of fire.

The wind picked up, and where small globs of the black stuff splattered, bare skin turned red and began to burn. They tried to rub it off. Blisters formed. They screamed and cursed and packed in tighter. It was like being jammed into the bridge all over again. The cloud pushed west.

☨

Franklin's survivors hurried past the medical tents to where long yellow school buses were
filling with people. A shake of Franklin's hand, a
pat on his back. "Thank you," they said quickly.
"The pilot—he leave so fast," Petre said in Russian,
"You thank him for us?" then, "Do svidaniya,"—
Goodbye, echoed Kat. Kone continued into the lot
without a word.

An old white sedan with several people inside
pulled up sharply. A young guy in a long heavy
coat rushed from the driver's side. Victoria smiled
at him as he moved behind her chair.

Head out the window, Kone returned in the
back of a black town car bearing U.S. government
plates. Asked if he could offer Walter van Patter a
lift. "No thank you, Mr. Kone," van Patter declined.
Kone's jaw bulged and he told the driver to move
on.

Clarence, the train engineer, the Russians, even
Mr. van Patter, found seats on one of the yellow
buses.

As Victoria's friend began to push her chair
away, she reached up, pulled Franklin's shoulder
down and kissed his cheek. "You did a wonderful
thing for us. Thank your brother for me, will you?"
She studied his face, "You're really a minister?"

"First Congregational Church, Erie, Pennsylvania," Franklin replied, feeling strangely warm
around the collar.

"You and the pilot—" she said. "Your hair's

so dark. He's so blond. You don't look much like brothers."

"We each share—a parent with Cynthia . . . " A lump formed in his throat. He looked down at Melissa in his arms, his niece's accusing eyes staring up at him. "We're both her uncles," he rasped.

The guy from the car rolled her to the rear side door, helped her from the wheelchair into the back seat. She looked back through the rear window as they drove away.

Harry—as Victoria had named him—was shaking inside Franklin's shirt. *I have to do something about this bird.*

Someone had left a cardboard box on the ground. Campbell's Chicken Soup. Inside was a stack of thin *USA TODAYs*. The headline read:

WHO'S RESPONSIBLE?

A computer-drawn image took up the whole first page. In his mind's eye he saw what no eye should ever see: an expanding fireball, bright and red and gold and lethal in all its evil glory. The blast was centered at Manhattan's south end—below *Wall Street,* labeled: *South Street Seaport.*

Balancing Melissa, Franklin slipped his free hand along the stack and set half the papers on the ground. He tugged out his front shirttails. Down inside his shirt, the owl's talons clung to the top of Franklin's pants. Harry didn't want to leave, the owl's speckled brown feathers shaking, shivering, all the way down the bird's fluffy white chest, his long feathery cape.

Franklin sucked in his abs and gently prised beneath the bird's talons with a finger, coaxing the owl into letting go. Finally, Harry released his grip and Franklin lifted him out of his shirt. Set him in the box.

The owl kept his large yellow eyes focused on Franklin as he scooped up the box in one arm, Melissa in the other. As Franklin hustled for the jet, spots of blood weeping across his shirtfront, Harry began a soft *"hup-hup-hup."*

37

The Bird

There's another one! Sal thought . . . *And another one . . .*

Along the highway berm were stranded cars with no apparent damage.

"I think they're running out of gas!" he said softly.

"How are *we*, Saly?" Margarete asked. "Will we make it to Momma's?"

Sal glanced at the Chevy's gauges. "Eighth of a tank," he muttered. "I don't know." They were up to forty. *At least we're moving again. Another hour should do it.* Margarete dialed in a local radio station.

> "Evacuees who try to return before their home areas are officially open are being blocked by military personnel; they will be required to turn their vehicles around. Those not yet allowed to go home may have

to spend another grueling night in
their cars."

"What's an evacee, Daddy?" their son asked.

"Listen!" Margarete shushed. The station's voice
continued,

"Traffic is still extreme. Apparently
some drivers unable to take the
stress have flatly refused to move.
The Army is using giant transport
trucks to shove any such cars aside.

"Soldiers were forced to return
fire on one man with a handgun who
died after receiving two bullets to the
head—"

Sal turned it off. "Those poor bastards." Not
even a glare from Margarete. "We're lucky we got
out when we did."

"When are they going to figure out who's behind
this, Saly?" Rita asked, echoing the very thing he'd
been thinking. She had a way of doing that.

As they came off the freeway the engine quit
for a moment, then restarted. Sal ran a red light.
When they turned onto Momma Conti's street the
engine stopped running completely.

They coasted into the driveway.

Their arrival was a complete surprise to Momma
Conti.

"Oh, my children," Daniella exclaimed as she
opened the door. It was the first time Sal had ever

heard such desperation in his mother-in-law's voice. Almost as if she included him in her affection.

"Oh, darling," Margarete's mother gushed all over her daughter. "And you drove *that car!*" An eyeball glanced at Sal. "I'm so relieved to see you. The news said there are no airlines, no trains at all east of Buffalo. And my two little pumpkins!" she knelt down, arms reaching out to hug the kids. "I'm so glad we're all together."

"Hello, Daniella."

"Hello, Sal." She turned back to Margarete.

"There was no way to call you!" Margarete said. "When the sirens started and the power went off—*we hadn't planned*—we barely had any food. We packed everything we had."

"Don't worry," Daniella said to her daughter, Sal thought eyeing him a bit snidely. "Momma has no electricity at the moment. But *our* food's still cold. Plenty for *everybody.*"

Margarete kissed her mother's cheek and turned to the kids. "Time for you two to have a quick bite and get to bed."

But the moment the kids were down, the power came on. For how long, Sal couldn't say. "They're transmitting from New York!" Daniella called.

The first thing Sal saw on his mother-in-law's television was a man with an owl's head sticking out of his shirt.

"That bird!"

Sal ran out of the room like a nut—*Who cares! Daniella already thinks so anyway*—to the room the kids were using, silently slid out the yellow toolbox by its black handle. Flipped up the lid, pawing through, dumping his daughter's dolls onto the floor—

There! Narrow brown stripes painted in streaks across its entire length . . .

Rita and her mother, staring at him as he ran back in. He held the feather to the television screen.

It's the same!

He could still picture the restaurant's dock. *That Middle Eastern man with the boat. Letting go of that bird beneath the Brooklyn Bridge.*

And then the picture was suddenly replaced by snow, the sound by static.

38

Hunt's Desperation

A giant of a helicopter roared in low overhead. The largest Franklin had ever seen—long and fat.

Suspended beneath on four cables was slung a semi-truck container. Its crisp white paint job, like that on the chopper, bore a huge red WILLIAMS POWER logo on its side. The amount of air the giant moved as it passed was like a small windstorm.

Franklin walked faster until he was up with Everon and Chuck again. "I thought you wanted to get out of here? That black mist looks like it's crossing the river," Franklin pointed.

But Everon wasn't listening.

The helicopter descended near the end of the row of big tents.

"Shouldn't we—"

"Hold on," Everon barked.

Soldiers ran over, unhooked cables, opened doors on the semi container's front and rear. They pulled out heavy wires, ran them to one of the hospital tents. A motor cranked up. Bright lights came on. *Emergency diesel generator*, Franklin realized.

But as the huge helicopter banked away, the air it moved didn't calm. Now it was gusty. The wind was picking up again.

"Everon!" waved a tall salt-and-pepper-haired man in a dark suit from the door of their Lear.

"Hunt?" Everon called out.

Hunt Williams, Franklin figured.

"I see you brought one of your backup generators." Everon studied the soldiers operating its controls. "Need to find out what's going on with it?" he added doubtfully.

"The Army asked me to bring it," Hunt said, "but no, my pilot could have handled this without me. I came here to talk to you."

"Me?" Everon and Chuck rolled the stretcher up against the Learjet's side door.

Hunt threw a questioning glance at the charred cocoon as they pushed it back into the jet's passenger area.

"My sister and her husband," Everon said. "We found them on the Upper East Side."

"Oh. I'm very sorry," Hunt said.

From somewhere along the taxiway Everon had obtained what appeared to be a large rubber—*a body bag*, Franklin realized. He watched Everon unfold it alongside the bulging Aztec blanket and push one edge underneath, his jaw clamped together, tugging its zipper back and forth between the charred blanket and the jet's floor.

Chuck moved in to help lift one side of the co-coon, but Everon gently moved the big man's arm away as if to say, *"I have this."*

Chuck stood there, silently watching. Franklin couldn't.

He scooted Harry's soup box back beneath the jet's small side table. Harry slanted his head up at Andréa. She was flipping quickly through a bunch of charts, pulling more from a pouch next to the pilot's seat.

Franklin took the seat next to her. Melissa let out a wail.

"Oh! Who's this?"

To a shocked Andréa, Franklin explained as briefly as possible how and where they'd found Melissa in the city.

"How long has she been wearing that?"

"Eighteen hours maybe? I don't know."

Andréa put away the maps.

Together they peeled off his niece's soiled pink nightsuit. Andréa wrapped a strip of what looked like part of a blue airline blanket between Melissa's legs, then doubled over the rest and wrapped Melissa up in it, cleverly finishing the job with several strips of white medical tape. *Who's going to take care of her now?* Franklin wondered. *Grandma Del, I guess.*

Andréa pulled out some milk to warm up in the jet's microwave.

"Don't give her that," Chuck said.

He fished a short disposable bottle and a can of baby formula out of his big green case. "Here."

A few minutes later Melissa was greedily sucking it down.

Franklin threw a handful of airline peanuts into Harry's soup box.

With Melissa slurping softly, Harry answering in his soft *"hup-hup-hup-hup,"* Franklin let his eyes close. *We have to get out of here,* he thought. *That cloud is coming.*

"Andréa says you have time in a Gulfstream?" he heard Hunt ask.

"Uh-huh," Everon grunted, like he was trying to force the middle of the bag past something.

Probably that damn piece of metal, Franklin thought.

"Obviously all the generating plants surrounding the city are out," Hunt said, "—from Long Island, to over here in New Jersey. What nobody expected was Llanerch, Mercer, Schuylkill, that we'd have so much system damage all the way down through—"

"What? *In Pennsylvania?* How far?" Everon grunted, struggling. "I remember you buying this for them, Bro." Everon wasn't talking to Hunt now. "A house-warming gift for Steve and Cyn, wasn't it?"

There it was again, Franklin could still see it— *that Aztec blanket waving in the Pacific roadside Baja breeze.* The thick tightly woven wool in orange and scarlet, forest green and lime—lots of lemon and turquoise.

"And now look at it," Everon spat out, "all burned and charred."

Franklin listened to his brother's breathing.

The pain there had nothing to do with a damaged blanket. Only what was wrapped inside.

When Everon had been quietly working the bag's zipper underneath again for half a minute or so, Hunt answered, "We don't know exactly how far—the damage runs at least halfway across the state."

"Did Ted and Stu stick around for the rest of the convention?" Everon asked, worry lines creasing his forehead.

"Yes," Hunt answered bitterly.

Everon said nothing.

"And now the President's ordered the nuclear plants shut down," Hunt said.

"He has? Why would he do something like that?"

"He's worried about a bomb hitting one of the reactors."

"It was a sea attack, wasn't it?"

"Looks that way."

"What an idiot."

Hunt nodded. "Gas stations can't pump gas. Hospitals and prisons are on their emergency generators."

"Uh—speaking of hospitals, I better get back," Chuck said softly.

The Aztec cocoon was in. Everon slowly zipped up the bag. The wind blew stronger. Franklin felt the plane move as Everon stepped outside. It felt like something darkened the sun.

"That cloud's coming in, Hunt," he heard Everon say. Then, "I don't know how we can ever thank you."

Why would someone do this? Franklin wondered.

Killing so many with the push of a button, however it was done. Franklin kept seeing his sister's smile, a smile he would never see again. Climbing and Cynthia's love of history had been her own links with Franklin. He was sure Everon already felt the loss of Cynthia's silly humor, popping up at the oddest times. The greatest sister who ever lived.

"No problem." Chuck's voice.

Strangers, people the killers would never meet. How could someone even think that way? Franklin wondered. *Whoever did this, there's no punishment, no form of death bad enough.*

Part of him wanted to see the person behind it burning over a spit of fire, twisting painfully—skin bubbling, hair shriveling—chunks of flesh burning off their bones. *To watch their blood boil as their marrow exploded into that last vestige of withering consciousness.*

Franklin opened his eyes, suddenly realizing Chuck had gone. *I didn't even thank him? What am I doing thinking like that?*

He jumped from the plane and dodged through the milling crowd.

"Chuck! Chuck, wait!"

Chuck turned around, startled.

"Thanks a lot, my friend," Franklin said, giving the big man a one-armed hug.

"No problem," he said bashfully. "Other circumstances, I'd have said I enjoyed it. Glad to do something useful."

The big man walked away.

So many refugees, Franklin thought, unable to

avoid bumping shoulders on his way back. *How are they going to get out of here before the cloud comes?*

Inside the plane, Hunt was unfolding a large white map. "Take a quick look at this copy of our power grid . . . *Everon?*"

Everon, stepped outside, looked at the sky, turned and quickly climbed back in, a scowl on his face. "We have to get out of here, Hunt."

"I understand, what I'm trying to say is . . . "

Franklin turned to Andréa. "Could you watch Melissa for me?" He glanced at the owl. "Keep an eye on Harry? Just for a couple of minutes? We need to find some people to fill up this plane."

"No problem."

"Six, max!" Everon called after him. "And make it really quick, Bro!"

39

A Dangerous Sample

Franklin hurried along the hospital tents. "Anyone want a ride to Nevada? We're flying out in a few minutes." He found half a dozen people wanting to go.

He was ready to head back when his eye caught on the old Pelican.

The files in Cynthia's cabinet! The last remnant of his sister's life. *I should have grabbed them. I should have brought them with us!*

At the Pelican's open cargo door, Franklin raised an open hand and held it over one of Cynthia's big crazy plastic flowers on the cabinet's side. He wished he could take the whole damn thing. It was too big.

Only the second drawer from the bottom was unlocked. The one he'd found Melissa in. He grabbed up the papers inside, the last few remaining scraps of Cynthia's life.

They were nearly swept from his arms. The sound of whirling blades grew in the air. Three light-gray helicopters with U.S. military markings set down right beside him. Even before their blades stopped turning, their pilots were on the ground.

Running away?

There were no passengers, Franklin realized. No one had been rescued.

Chuck's radiation counter was under the Pelican's port-side seat. Cynthia's papers under one arm, he turned it on and moved to the nearest Army helicopter, leaving the audio knob turned down. Its needle swung intermittently.

He probed the bottom of the chopper's windshield where a small amount of dark watery goop had collected. The needle arced halfway across the dial. *Radiation! They've been rained on. Too hot to risk bringing out any more survivors!*

Franklin's long dark hair lifted lightly off his neck. With a lover's touch, air drifted across his cheeks. It was, he knew, the coming breath of death. The cloud was coming.

He swung the probe to where a clot of gray powder clung to the helicopter's landing strut. The meter slammed hard right off the scale. The gray stuff was deadly!

Later he would wonder what possessed him.

On the ground nearby lay a small empty water bottle. Working the lip of the bottle gingerly back and forth, he scooped up a tiny sample of the gray goo. He held the bottle's bottom uncomfortably, watching the stuff cling to the inside of the bottle's neck. Careful not to shake the sample down near his fingers, he spun the cap back on.

He was winding a gray scarf that blew by the helicopter around the bottle, when he heard a voice yell, *"Hey!* Get away from there!"

He'd been noticed!

He backpedaled away from the choppers, turned and ran between two jets.

"Hey!" another voice yelled after him.

40

A Drop Of Rain

Gasping for breath Franklin fell through the jet's door. "I think the military's after me!"

"*Wha—why?*" Andréa asked.

"I took a radioactive sample off one of their helicopters."

"*Are you nuts?*" she shook her head. "*Both of you!*" exasperated. "We better get going."

"I found a family who wanted a ride. Where—" Franklin looked into the jet's empty passenger area. Everon, Hunt, even the black body bag, were gone.

"You're taking Mr. Williams' Gulfstream home," Andréa explained. "And you're taking a bunch of refugees out west with you."

Franklin hurried Cynthia's papers into the soup box next to Harry. Gently shoving the bird aside, he squeezed in the radiation counter. Put the sample in the corner farthest from Harry.

Andréa carried Melissa; Franklin, Harry's box.

When Andréa got more than a couple feet ahead of Franklin, Melissa and the owl began to let out cries and howls. They really didn't like being separated.

Andréa led Franklin to a long white aircraft at the end of the row. He could see Everon through the cockpit window talking rapidly with a tall, thin man dressed in airline whites.

A young Hispanic woman lurched after her small son out the jet's open door. A pear-shaped old woman with white hair and a bald old man followed. They bent over heaving red and green bile. The little boy and his mother went to their knees.

The old woman stopped first and put a hand on the young woman's back, looked up at Franklin. "I'm afraid," she coughed, "you'll have to go without us. They were *snowed* on. Got us too."

"Snow? Did it snow?"

"That gray stuff. They had it all over their shoes. We think the kid ate some," she coughed. "On the way here, over in Queens—" gulping as if she was about to let loose again, "—we got hit with that stinging black crap out of the sky." Her teary eyes turned to the short bald man next to her. "Let's get Cheri and Johnny to a hospital tent, Louie."

Franklin shook his head as they staggered away.

> *"And behold," he mumbled, "a pale green horse: and Hell and pestilence followed with him. And the names of they that sat on them was Death."*

He turned suddenly to Melissa. *Will she get sick too?* She'd been outside in that cabinet all night long.

A hint of wind from the city forced its way between the jets. Franklin looked up. The black mist was right *THERE!* Maybe a mile away. Coming in fast.

A man and woman ran up, pulling a little boy and girl by their hands. "Is this the plane going to Nevada?" the man asked.

"Uh, yes it is."

Franklin followed them onboard as Everon glanced at him and said to the man in airline whites, "Here's my co-pilot now."

It looked like word had gotten around. People squooshed over to make room to let the little family of newcomers buckle in. The whole back of the plane was full. To the stares of several passengers, Franklin set Harry's soup box on the floor, hurried past leather seats filled with refugees.

Back in cargo he stepped around the fat rubber body bag. It was strapped to the floor with some of his climbing rope. There was a small plastic window on top—like something that would hold a shipping label.

The words read: Certificate Of Death.

That sense of directionless rage welled up in him again—unlike anything he'd ever felt—the urge to strike at anything. *Not anymore! I'm a minister, for Christ's sake!*

Franklin found an empty upper compartment and shoved the scarf-wrapped bottle inside. When he got back up front, he took Melissa from Andréa then leaned into the cockpit between Everon and the man in airline whites.

"We've swapped jets," Everon said. "I've agreed to help Hunt fix—where were you?"

"I was getting Cynthia's papers. We've got to get off the East Coast!"

"Did you see that wind? It's almost too late to leave. I don't know if we should be in the air when the next—whatever's coming hits. If—"

"It may be too dangerous to stay! Three Army helicopters just landed back from Manhattan. They came back radioactive. They had to have been in the fallout zone."

"Maybe that's why the military wouldn't let us south of—"

Franklin pointed. "There's another reason we'd better get out of here."

A horde of people were coming down the road, like all Manhattan was on its way. Poorly dressed homeless people alongside Wall Street types, others in bathrobes.

"We may have shot ourselves in the foot, Bro," Everon nodded, "opening that bridge." He looked to the man in airline whites.

The man grabbed his flight bag and left the co-pilot's seat. "We're all set. Mr. Williams wants a quick word."

Once the Williams man was out, Franklin frowned and asked, "This thing's pretty big. It only takes one pilot to fly it?"

"*Shhhh!* It's not usually legal," Everon whispered,

"but all standard FAA regulations are temporarily suspended. All flights are subject to military approval under martial law. In other words, it all depends on whether we can get clearance. I can handle it just fine myself—as long as nothing breaks and things don't get too crazy."

Franklin and Melissa followed Everon off the plane.

"One thing—" Hunt began.

Everon looked at his own right shoulder. A dime-sized drop of something dark and thick and wet had fallen on his jacket collar. He glanced at the sky. Moved a finger to touch the stuff.

"Don't!" Franklin said.

The middle of the heavy black cloud was right over their heads.

Franklin leaned into the jet, pulled Chuck's meter out of Harry's box. Turned it on. Waved it around Everon's collar.

"Radioactive!"

Everon jerked off his jacket, threw it to the ground. "Let's get out of here!"

The daylight dimmed. A blast of wind came through, gusting violently, then died.

"One thing—" Hunt rushed as Everon stepped through the big jet's doorway.

"What?"

"Please. No *barrel rolls* in the Gulfstream."

ᴘ

"Second, our job is to control debris!" Colonel

Marsh explained. "What search quadrant were you flying?"

"Seventy-second street. West side. Uh, sir, it's getting pretty damned hot, even up there."

"Mueller's just yellow!" a second pilot spat through clenched teeth.

"Sir," the first pilot shot back, "it's raining atomic fallout over there! If we fly another mission we're in danger of being poisoned. We absorbed more that last flight through the chopper's skin than all our other missions combined!"

"No reason we can't wear radiation suits," the second pilot shot back.

"How are we supposed *to fly* in a rad-suit, sir?"

General Anders roared up in an old staff car, one of the few still working. Shaven head, long military coat with sheepskin collar. He flew from the back seat.

"Report, Colonel."

Marsh began explaining the progress with the tents, power and hospital facilities. The radiation picked up by the last three helicopters he'd sent in.

"Perhaps we ought to relocate our hospital facilities back some," Anders agreed.

"Colonel!" The third pilot blurted as he ran up out of breath. "Unauthorized personnel snooping around our helicopters!" He swallowed and before Marsh could respond, added, "Uh—with what looked like a radiation counter!"

"We cannot have civilians taking radiation readings off our helicopters!"

"Uh, excuse me, Colonel Marsh, General." A

sergeant had been standing by, leaning foot to foot like he had to go to the bathroom. Anders' and Marsh's eyes shot to him. "I—I'm not sure," he said hesitantly, "I think I saw him too. He scooped some dirt off the landing gear of one chopper into a water bottle—"

"What!" Anders yelled. "We can't have that! Arrest him!"

"Yes sir. He disappeared somewhere into the row of jets here. I spoke to the same guy earlier this morning. He said he came on a Williams jet."

"Describe him."

"Long dark hair. Leather jacket. Blue eyes."

"Well, search every single aircraft if you have to. Start on this end and work your way back."

"There's a big Williams Gulfstream up a little ways," one of Marsh's men said.

"That minister at the gate this morning, Sarge?" another man put in.

"You seen him?" the sergeant barked.

"He just got into that small Lear up at the beginning of the row. The one with *Williams* painted on it. I went past a minute ago and the door was closed. I think it's leaving for the runway right now."

Anders turned to Marsh. "I want three men."

"Sergeant Rodriquez," Marsh commanded, "you, Bell and Zimmer follow the general's staff car . . . "

☩ ☨

Holding Melissa in his lap, Franklin looked back through the cockpit door at the people traveling with them. Fourteen children and adults were belted to the white leather seats. There was a sense they were consciously avoiding the luggage door that shielded the wide black rubber bag—the way the parents had placed their kids away from the aisle.

The owl was shaking.

A single worry pushed the rest away: *This owl looks pretty sick—that young woman, her little boy, the two old people who brought them too. Will Melissa be next?*

He watched the jet two ahead turn onto the runway and accelerate to takeoff speed. Two old green staff cars with large stars on their doors sped down the opposite taxiway.

"What're *they* doing?" Everon said.

The cars crossed the runway and stopped abruptly at Hunt's smaller Lear, two jets back. Soldiers jumped from the cars. One banged on the Learjet's door.

"That's General Anders. And that security guard Vandersommen is with him!"

"They think we're in there," Everon said. *"Whoa!"* Bushes whipped around outside, then bent over. Just as suddenly, all was still.

"I—I think they might actually be looking for me," Franklin said.

Globs of black pelted across the jet's windshield. *Big sloppy chunks.*

Franklin leaned forward to see back through the cockpit window. It was falling all over the wings.

"Will the jet take off with that stuff on it?" he

asked. "I remember you saying even a little snow can really cut a plane's lift. That stuff looks a lot heavier than a little snow."

"Unless it slides off. It increases the required runway length. A bunch. *And* we're fully loaded."

Franklin grabbed Chuck's meter. He extended its probe. Waved it around the cockpit's ceiling and walls. "It's radioactive! The windshield's off the scale! What do we do?"

Without waiting for a change in clearance, Everon made an illegal turn onto a runway access closer than the one assigned, braked the big jet and keyed his mic.

"Gulfstream—Five-Five-Six-Six-Sierra-Whiskey to Teterboro tower. Ready to depart Runway Two-Four."

For many, many miles the second fish had been swimming patiently beneath the water's surface. Nowhere near its planned destination, its nose hammered directly into shore. To the fish's small but potent brain, the impact made one thing clear:

It had arrived.

Eight shakes of a second later it became nothing more than a ball of pure expanding energy.

41

Jet Confusion

Hunt Williams' Learjet joined the line of those waiting to depart. Two old green staff cars roared along the taxiway and screeched to a stop beneath Hunt's wing. Out stormed General Anders.

Through the Lear's front window, Hunt watched Everon taxi the big Gulfstream into position. A moment later, the monstrous WILLIAMS helicopter came overhead and turned south.

A fist pounded on the Learjet's door. Hunt rose from his seat and opened the door himself.

"Mr. *Williams?*" Anders' face tight, eyes squinting. "What are you—? Who's in *your* plane?"

"Everon Student. He's going out west to pick up equipment and personnel."

"Out west? Where?" Anders asked.

"Nevada," Hunt replied. "Talk to him about it when he gets back. He's returning to Pennsylvania to work for me."

"When?"

"Tomorrow."

"Doing what?"

"Restoring my company's part of the power grid."

"Is there a dark-haired man in a black leather jacket with him?"

"Yes. Why?"

Big black blobs fell on the general's windshield, the plane's wings. A chunk of the stuff fell on the general's shoulder.

"What do you call that?" Hunt asked.

The general's eyes went big. *"Crap!"*

"Exactly." Without another word, Hunt stepped back and pulled the door.

Anders threw himself into his car, hand out. "Give me the mic!"

† ♱

There was no answer from the tower. Everon began to wonder, *will they clear us?* "Take that headset, Bro." He pointed to a switch. "Make sure everybody's buckled in tight."

"Please make certain your seat belts are secure," Franklin announced over the intercom, looking back into the cabin. Children held on parents' laps. Every seat was full.

A familiar controller's voice came over the radio. "Teterboro tower to Gulfstream Sierra-Whiskey—"

"Sue!" Everon whispered.

"Cleared for takeoff, Runway Two-Four. Have a safe flight."

Everon put a hand on the throttle, ready to push

up the engines, when a black kitten with matted fur skittered frightfully across the runway in front of them.

"How much worse can it get?" Franklin muttered to no one in particular.

"Probably a lot," Everon replied nodding to their right, and gave the big Gulf full throttle. Off the jet's right side a mob of thousands was climbing the airport fence. They disappeared behind.

Long seconds later, he eased back half an inch on the yoke. The jet didn't lift.

"What's going on?" Franklin asked.

"That goo's giving us a real problem," Everon said through clenched teeth, easing the yoke back still farther.

The runway ahead shrank to nothing.

ᚠ

"That flight never received military authorization," Anders shouted at the tower. "I understand they've got bodies in there! No one's seen their death certificates. And we can't have them spreading rumors of radioactivity scares and panicking people!"

"Your people approved the flight," The female voice radioed back.

"We thought it was Hunt Williams onboard. This is a direct violation of Emergency Executive Order 16-176. No unauthorized flights until national radar coverage has been re-established."

"Too late, sir." Anders' sergeant interrupted.

The big jet was already rolling, gaining speed.

"Goddammit!" Anders roared.

"Why isn't he lifting off?" the sergeant mumbled.

Ignoring him, Anders steeled back an angry retort then let out a blast of air.

"General, sir!" Colonel Marsh from the second car, braving the black chunks, tapped on the general's window. "Sir!"

Anders lowered the glass. "What is it?"

"We've lost all communications with Washington!"

"What?"

"I was talking to General Thompson's aide for you at the Pentagon and—they just weren't there anymore. It's like there's nothing there."

"Is it the satellite again?"

"I don't think so. It never came back."

� ⚚

With less than two hundred feet to spare, the Gulfstream's nose left the ground. The rear wheels weren't going to clear the airport boundary fence.

They did.

Everon felt like they missed the trees by inches. Immediately he banked west.

Straight into the nearest rain cloud he could find.

ᚹ

Vandersommen, the security guard who'd tried to prevent the brothers going in to rescue their family, stood on the Teterboro ramp watching the jet fly away as the first fat black drops came down.

The airport's conical red windsock rotated randomly. North. East. Then south. The windsock hung limp against the pole.

And then it *blew*.

General Anders' call to move had come too late. Tents flared and billowed in the cold increasing wind. Dark, gooey drops left stinging red marks on the skin of half a million Teterboro refugees.

Meters came out.

Radiation! A lot of it.

The black rain poured down. The cold dark water gathered in rivulets. The rivulets became streams that flowed through the tents, deadly even to the touch.

"Get out!" a confusion of voices exploded.

"Run!"

"Where?"

People locked themselves inside porta-potties that in minutes floated in the new lake then fell over sideways. Others stood on plastic milk boxes in the tents, anything they could find. People stopped worrying about treatment and simply tried to escape.

Yet some doctors and nurses stubbornly ignored the cold burning black as it flowed around their bare ankles. Continued triaging patients until they couldn't bear the pain, then joined their patients on gurneys, trying to wash down their own legs and ankles with bottles of saline.

In one of the tents, terror now gripped Cheri Enriquez. Pain in her joints, a dizzy, cold, sweaty kind of flu—realization set in. It was coming on so fast. This was not like any sickness she'd ever known. Among the scrambling crowd, she held Johnny against her knees in the burning mud. Maybe she deserved this sickness. She shouldn't have let old Mrs. Goodman talk her into leaving home. Maybe Jáime was looking for them. Making the sign of the cross, she puked out the last words that would ever leave her lips:

"But Johnny, God, why Johnny?"

☖ ♰

In seconds the brothers were hit by extreme turbulence—bouncing groans shook the plane.

The right wing dropped forty degrees or more. Everon struggled to bring it back up, over-correcting thirty degrees to the left. *BAM!* Turbulence hammered the wings in the opposite direction.

Franklin could see nothing through the windows. He felt his butt leave the seat, the seat belt tight across his lap, and nearly lost his hold on Melissa as his head hit the ceiling. "Can the plane take this?" he shouted, pulling his belt snug.

"It'll take it," Everon grunted, trying to pull the wings level again. "It'll have to. We have to get that stuff off."

"All this turbulence is from the cloud?"

"I—I don't know. I don't see how."

The right wing dropped again. Everon corrected

hard, yoke twisted full left. There was almost no effect. The cabin continued to rotate.

"No!"

But the air was not to be denied.

Over they went.

Franklin heard cries from the plane's rear. It was all he could do to hang onto Melissa. Harry flapped into the cabin air. The engine whined, its pitch rising. *BAM!* something hit the big jet.

Far in back a man held onto his young son by the strap of his blue jumper. Behind him the luggage door flew open. The wide black body bag slammed upward against the web of Franklin's climbing rope Everon had laced it down with.

The plane was upside down. Twisting metal screeched. *Bam! Bam! Bam! Bam!*

"Fuck it!" Everon shouted. Reversing the yoke, he accelerated the roll. Franklin could just make out the words uttered through his brother's clenched teeth. "Hunt's. Just. Going to have. To deal with it—"

The jet's lights went out. All of them.

All Franklin could hear as he felt the nose pitch down, hanging from his seat belt, clinging to Melissa, was a slamming sound and the dropping whine of the big jet's engines winding down.

**Find out what happens
to Franklin and Everon right away!**

**Go to StateOfReason.com
And enter *your code* for a special offer!**

144567

If you enjoyed LOSS OF REASON,
please go to Amazon.com
or your favorite review website
and leave the best review
you feel comfortable writing.

This is the second best way
to ensure the writers you *really* like
continue writing the type of books
you want to read.

The best, of course,
is to give a copy to your friends.

MILES A. MAXWELL IS OUT OF CHEYENNE, WYOMING.